SiXTY-EiGHT
ROOMS

2

·· STEALING MAGIC ··

Keep Reading !

2013,

MOM ≩ PAO

BOOKS BY MARIANNE MALONE

SiXTY-EiGHT
2 ROOMS

·· STEALING MAGiC ··

■ ■ ■

MARIANNE MALONE
ILLUSTRATIONS BY GREG CALL

A YEARLING BOOK

Text copyright © 2012 by Marianne Malone
Cover art and interior illustrations copyright © 2012 by Greg Call

Photography copyright © by The Art Institute of Chicago. Mrs. James Ward Thorne, American, 1882–1966, E-27: French Library of the Modern Period, 1930s, c. 1937, Miniature room, mixed media, Interior: 16 1/8 x 24 3/8 x 19 1/2 in. (40.3125 x 60.9375 x 48.75 cm), Scale: 1 inch = 1 foot, Gift of Mrs. James Ward Thorne, 1941.1212, The Art Institute of Chicago.

All rights reserved. Published in the United States by Yearling, an imprint of Random House Children's Books, a division of Random House, Inc., New York. Originally published in hardcover in the United States by Random House Children's Books, New York, in 2012.

Yearling and the jumping horse design are registered trademarks of Random House, Inc.

Visit us on the Web! randomhouse.com/kids

Educators and librarians, for a variety of teaching tools, visit us at RHTeachersLibrarians.com

The Library of Congress has cataloged the hardcover edition of this work as follows:
Malone, Marianne.
Stealing magic : a sixty-eight rooms adventure / Marianne Malone. — 1st ed.
p. cm.
Sequel to: The sixty-eight rooms.
Summary: Chicago sixth-graders Jack and Ruthie return to the Thorne Rooms at the Art Institute of Chicago and once again go back in time while trying to stop an art thief from endangering the miniature rooms.
ISBN 978-0-375-86819-1 (trade) — ISBN 978-0-375-96819-8 (lib. bdg.) — ISBN 978-0-375-86790-3 (trade pbk.) — ISBN 978-0-375-89872-3 (ebook)
1. Art Institute of Chicago—Juvenile fiction. [1. Art Institute of Chicago—Fiction. 2. Time travel—Fiction. 3. Miniature rooms—Fiction. 4. Size—Fiction. 5. Magic—Fiction.] I. Title.
PZ7.M29646St 2012
[Fic]—dc22
2011000074

Printed in the United States of America

10 9 8 7 6 5 4 3 2

First Yearling Edition 2013

TO ZACHARY AND JONAH,
for supplies of wit and charm

··· CONTENTS ···

SiXTY-EiGHT ROOMS

2

··STEALING MAGIC··

BREAKFAST AT RUTHIE'S

IT WAS SOMETIME BEFORE DAWN when Ruthie Stewart opened her eyes. The room around her appeared strangely dark without the usual stripes of streetlight filtering through the blinds. She sat up and rubbed her eyes, noticing that she was no longer sitting on her nice, soft bed, but rather on the cold, hard floor. She thought she had fallen out of bed, something she hadn't done since she was four years old. Her eyes began to adjust, and she could make out nothing familiar; she wasn't even in her bedroom. With an unnatural light coming from above, the walls around her came into focus as shiny and black. *What's going on?* She wanted to get out of this room—although it didn't feel like a room, more like a box—but, standing up and turning a full 360 degrees, she couldn't see any way out. Then a door appeared near the corner, and she wondered how she had missed seeing it. She ran through it and found herself in an almost identical room, completely empty, with shiny black walls and that peculiar glow from above. This room had slightly different dimensions, and the door she had just passed through seemed to disappear. *Where am I?* she kept repeating to herself. *There must be a way out.*

With increasing panic, she continued to look for doors, which appeared only after she had gone over every wall a few times. Finally she entered a room with white papers scattered all over the floor, glowing as they reflected the odd overhead light. She picked up a piece of paper and saw handwriting—it looked like Jack's—but she could read only one sentence: *Get me out.* The rest was certainly written in English, but she couldn't make out any of the other words. At first she could see the letters clearly, but then they became foggy and unfocused. She picked up another piece of paper. *Ah—this one I can read!* But no sooner had she read *Get me out* than the following letters became unreadable. She threw the paper to the floor and tried again and then again. She was becoming more frustrated by the second and was ready to stomp out, but, unlike in all the other rooms, no door appeared through which to leave. All she could think was, *Get* me *out!* Suddenly the light from above seemed to dim, and she had the horrible sense that soon she would be enveloped in complete, claustrophobic darkness. Anxiety spread from deep in her stomach all the way out to her fingertips. Inky blackness surrounded her.

With a jolt, Ruthie sat upright in her bed. She was hot all over and breathing rapidly, so she tried to take a deep, cleansing breath. With her knees pulled up to her chest, she shuddered a little.

She glanced across the pile of stuff on her sister's desk to see that the clock read 5:15 a.m.—too early to get up. Claire, lightly snoring, looked peaceful as she slept. Moments like this made Ruthie glad she had to share a room. The streetlight coming through the blinds sketched lines on the far wall, crossing over the posters and bulletin board. All this calmed Ruthie, and she lay back down, wondering why she had had such a scary dream. Everything had been so wonderful and exciting the day before.

As she tried to fall back asleep, she pictured last night's party in her head. The gallery opening of Mr. Bell's exhibition had been such fun. Ruthie leaned over and felt under her bed for the box in which she stashed important stuff. She lifted the lid and took out the newspaper clipping from a couple of months ago that had first reported the amazing find. She reread her favorite lines:

> Ruthie Stewart and Jack Tucker (son of painter Lydia Tucker), students in the sixth grade at Oakton School, made an important discovery in the world of art photography. Collectors in the city may well remember the work of Edmund Bell, famous for his portraits of artists and others in Chicago's African American community, and

how his work seemed to vanish twenty-three years ago, ending his promising career. While the sixth graders were helping a friend, local book dealer Minerva McVittie, sort through unopened boxes from long-past estate sales and auctions, they came across a photo album. Stewart and Tucker had recently met Edmund Bell at the Art Institute, where he works as a guard, and learned of the lost photos. When they saw the album in a box buried deep in McVittie's storeroom, they recognized its importance. "This is a one-in-a-million event," a local art dealer commented. "We can all thank Miss Stewart and Mr. Tucker for not missing the significance of what they'd come across."

Of course, what the article didn't say, and what nobody knew but Ruthie, Jack, and Mrs. McVittie, was that the album had not been found in her storeroom. They couldn't tell reporters the whole truth—mostly because nobody would believe them. How could they explain about the magic they had stumbled upon? First, there was the key that Jack had found, created by Duchess Christina of Milan in the sixteenth century. Second, this key enabled Ruthie to shrink and enter the Thorne Rooms, the sixty-eight miniature rooms in the Art Institute perfectly crafted by Narcissa Thorne more than half a century ago. Third, the magic—which they later learned could work on Jack too as long as he was holding Ruthie's hand—let them go back and forth in time. And last, in a miniature sixteenth-century English room, they had found Mr. Bell's album, shrunk and hidden inside a very old cabinet!

Finding the key and Mr. Bell's lost photographs had been the biggest adventure of Ruthie's life; it wasn't just exciting, it was important. Ruthie and Jack believed that the secret of the key must be protected, so it was a big responsibility to guard this powerful magic. And the whole experience made Ruthie feel that something extraordinary had finally happened to her.

She put the article back and placed the box under her bed again. She rested her head on her pillow, imagining herself back in bed in the room where she had found the album. Closing her eyes, she saw the green silk canopy high overhead, the vines and birds in the patterned fabric, her fingers stroking the smooth sheets. Her breathing slowed, and before she knew it, her mother was waking her for breakfast.

"Let me sleep." Ruthie's voice was muffled by her pillow.

"Sweetie, it's already ten-thirty!" her mother answered. "It's not healthy to sleep so late."

"I need my sleep," Ruthie grumbled back.

"I hope you're not coming down with something," her mother said worriedly. "Let's see how you feel after you've had some breakfast." She went back to the kitchen.

The tinny, irritating sound of Claire's cell phone punctured what was left of the morning quiet. Claire ran into the room and lunged for her phone. She said hello in a dreamy voice.

"Claire, can't you talk somewhere else?" Ruthie groused.

"No, and you should get up anyway."

Ruthie realized it was no use. The day had begun.

She shuffled into the bathroom and closed the door. She couldn't hear her sister's weirdly syrupy voice from in there. It was strange to think how her practical, serious sister turned into another person when she talked to her new boyfriend. Whom did it remind her of? She thought about how Sophie, the French girl they'd met outside a room from eighteenth-century France, had batted her eyelashes—at Jack, of all people! That picture in her head helped clear the sleep fog from her brain, and she smiled at herself in the mirror. The unease and anxiety she had felt in the middle of the night lessened a bit, but she couldn't rid herself of it completely. She brushed her teeth and ran a comb through her hair.

"Good morning, sleepyhead." Her dad kissed the top of her head as he passed her at the kitchen table. The smell of butter browning filled the air. They didn't always have spectacular food at her house, not like at Jack's, where his mother treated cooking like another form of art. But sometimes, on weekends or special occasions, her parents went all out. Ruthie's dad's breakfast specialty was pancakes. Her mother's was crepes, and this morning she was cooking. She stood at the stove, still in her pajamas and bathrobe, expertly flipping the golden disks. A stack of them already sat on a plate in the middle of the table. Ruthie took one, spooned some strawberry jam onto the delicate, lacy circle, rolled it up, and took her first bite. It melted in her mouth.

She had just taken another bite when her father said, "You must have been exhausted from last night—you never sleep this late."

"I was up in the middle of the night," Ruthie answered out of her crepe-filled mouth.

"Did you have a bad dream?" her mom asked.

Ruthie chewed the last bite and then swallowed. "Yeah, it was weird. It was something about being stuck in some kind of dark maze." As she said that, it dawned on her: it wasn't a maze at all. It was Jack's bento box—the shiny black lacquer box from Japan with several compartments, which he'd used as a lunchbox and which they'd left, shrunk, in the Japanese room! But she couldn't tell her parents that. "I felt kinda trapped."

Her description of the dream was interrupted as Claire's laugh rang through the apartment, all the way from behind the closed bedroom door. Ruthie and her dad gave each other the same knowing look.

"It appears Gabe is Mr. Charming," her dad said.

"He seems nice enough," her mom responded.

"I get kicked out of my room when he calls. Which is all the time now," Ruthie complained.

"That doesn't seem like fair treatment for a local celebrity, does it?" Her father handed her the morning newspaper. "Look—the party was covered, complete with color pictures."

Sure enough, on the first page of the Arts section, last night's opening of Mr. Bell's exhibition rated four photos, including one of Ruthie, Jack, Mrs. McVittie and Edmund Bell, all beaming.

"I can't believe it's such a big deal," Ruthie marveled. As she filled, folded, and ate two more crepes, she inspected her image on the page: not the greatest photo of her, but not too bad. Mrs. McVittie stood next to her at almost the same height, clutching her small beaded hand-bag, which glistened in the photographer's flash. In her morning grogginess, Ruthie had forgotten that her new treasure lay waiting in her top drawer. She shoved another crepe into her mouth in a hurry.

"It was so generous of Minerva to give you that beautiful handbag, Ruthie," her mom said. "Where did you put it?"

"My top drawer."

"I'll get you some tissue paper to wrap it in," her mother said. But Ruthie's mind had already shifted to a mix of thoughts, her bad dream foremost among them. Looking at the newspaper photos triggered the unease that simmered just under the surface of what should have been a really good mood. She'd better call Jack.

"Thanks for the crepes, Mom." Ruthie pushed back from the table.

In her room, Ruthie dug in her backpack to find her phone. With her sister gabbing on hers and hogging their room, Ruthie decided to claim the bathroom. She could call Jack from there; she didn't want anyone to hear the conversation.

Ruthie pushed the speed-dial number for Jack. It rang and rang. Finally, on the ninth ring, he picked up.

"Hey, Ruthie," he said in a sleepy but cheery voice. "What time is it?"

"It's just after eleven."

"Cool. That was a great party last night."

"Yeah—we're in the paper this morning."

"Very cool. I'll see if we got it yet."

"Wait, Jack. Before you do that, I have to tell you something. I had a nightmare last night. I think it was about your bento box."

"How could the bento box be scary?"

"Easy—if it's giant-sized, and you're trapped in it, which I was. And then all these pieces of paper with your handwriting on them were scattered everywhere, only I couldn't read most of them except one part that said *Get me out*."

Jack was silent on the other end.

"What do you think it means?" she finally prompted him.

"I don't know," he said, which Ruthie thought was an unsatisfactory response. "What do *you* think it means?"

"I think I'm worried that we left it in the Japanese room. Maybe it was too risky. Do you think leaving it there with the letter in it was a bad idea?"

"I hadn't really thought about it that way. But now that you mention it, yeah, I guess it could cause trouble, like if the wrong kind of person finds it."

"When we left it, I was only thinking that people like us might find it—you know, other kids. But anyone could find it."

The line was quiet for a few seconds as the two of them came to terms with this new dilemma. Jack broke the silence.

"What are you doing today?"

"I don't know yet," Ruthie answered.

"I'm coming over," Jack said.

When Ruthie, now dressed, reentered the kitchen, her dad was putting on his coat.

"I invited Mrs. McVittie over for brunch. I'm going to get her and walk her here. Want to keep me company?" he asked.

"I'll wait here—Jack's coming over."

"And Gabe is coming to get me," Claire said. She was looking at the paper, drinking coffee. She had just started that habit. Ruthie thought it seemed strange, as if her sister was trying to look older. "Hey, did anyone see this article?" Claire asked. "There's an art thief on the loose!"

Claire read aloud from the first paragraph.

> Local art collectors are on edge over a surge in art thefts in the Chicago area. Police suspect the crime spree is the work of a single thief. Victims have reported no missing electronics or other items usually sought by burglars. Instead, only

single items, usually small paintings, sculptures,
and objets d'art, have been reported missing.
Chicago police have no leads and ask collectors
to exercise measures to protect their valuables.

"I wonder if Mrs. McVittie knows about this," Ruthie
said.

"All I know is we'll need more crepes!" Ruthie's mom
said. "Here, Ruthie, you flip a few while I get dressed."

Her mother made flipping the crepes look easy! She
had taught Ruthie how to do it, but Ruthie wasn't so good
at it yet. She stood there watching the light yellow batter
turn golden around the edges while little air holes formed
and popped. Timing was everything. If she waited too
long, the crepe would burn; if she flipped too soon, it
would stick to the pan and she'd end up with a crumpled
mess. She gave the pan a little shake, and the crepe slid a
bit—time to flip. She held the pan with two hands and
gave a slight outward and upward thrust. Like an Olympic
gymnast, the disk lifted, turned over and landed perfectly
in the pan.

"Not bad," Claire said from behind her coffee cup.

"Thank you, thank you." Ruthie took a bow. As soon as
a crepe was done she slid it onto the plate. She was happy
to have this task; she could give it all of her attention while
she waited for Jack to arrive. She successfully made a dozen
more crepes.

When the door buzzer sounded, the two sisters ran to

push the intercom button, saying hello in unison. Gabe's voice answered back.

Ruthie groaned.

"What are you so antsy about?" Claire asked, buzzing him in. "Don't be annoying while Gabe's here, okay?"

Ruthie didn't answer as she went back to the stove. She had more important things on her mind, like what was taking Jack so long. She drizzled the last of the batter into the crepe pan and watched the color slowly darken, not noticing her own tapping foot.

"Hey, Ruthie." Gabe walked into the kitchen. "How's it going?"

"Fine." Ruthie moved the pan out and up in perfect form—almost. This time she tossed the crepe too high, making it turn not once but one and a half times, and it landed folded over on itself in the pan. Her cheeks burned as she turned to the sink. Fortunately, her mom came into the kitchen at that moment.

"Good morning, Gabe," she said.

"Hi, Mrs. Stewart," he answered.

"Good job, Ruthie! Looks like I can retire as head crepe maker around here," she said, admiring the full stack of fresh crepes on the table, not noticing the one going into the garbage disposal at that very moment.

Finally the door buzzer sounded again, and Ruthie bounded for it. She slammed the intercom button.

"Hey, it's me." Jack's voice came through the speaker.

Ruthie buzzed him in before he finished the short sentence.

"What took you so long?" Ruthie demanded when he appeared in the doorway.

"I just got up, remember?" Jack looked at her as though she were slightly crazed and then noticed the telltale smell of fresh crepes. He walked right into the kitchen smiling at everyone.

"Good morning, Jack," Ruthie's mom said. "Pull up a chair."

"Wait. First come see what Mrs. McVittie gave me last night." Ruthie yanked him out of the kitchen and into her room. She closed the door.

"I'm really freaked out," Ruthie began. "It's like my dream was some kind of premonition. I feel like it was telling me to do something important, but I don't know what!"

Jack remained calm, as usual. "What did you want to show me?"

"Oh, right." She turned to her bureau and opened the top drawer. There among the socks lay the beaded handbag, gleaming brightly in contrast with the mostly dull socks.

"Isn't it beautiful?"

Jack was underwhelmed. "It's a purse," he said flatly.

"It's an antique. Mrs. McVittie said it belonged to her sister. Last night when we were walking home, I thought I felt it warming up in my hand."

Jack took the small bag in his own hands for a closer inspection. "Did it only happen once?" He handed it back to her. "What about now? Do you feel anything?"

She held it carefully and tried to sense the temperature. Was it warming in her hand? Was it glowing too brightly in the indoor lighting of her bedroom? She shook her head. "No, nothing. I probably imagined it."

From out in the apartment the two of them heard everyone welcoming Mrs. McVittie.

"Let's go to the museum today," Jack suggested. "At least to take a look at the Japanese room and my bento box."

"Okay," Ruthie agreed. "But we'd better go out and say hello."

Ruthie gave Mrs. McVittie a hug as soon as she saw her. The kitchen was too small for all the people who squeezed around the table. Ordinarily Ruthie would have enjoyed a Sunday morning like this, but now she just wanted to rush to the museum and check on the bento box!

The crepes had been devoured and the newspaper had been passed around the table several times before Jack saw the article about the art thief. "Mrs. McVittie, have you read this?" he asked. "It says some pretty important art collections have been hit."

"Yes, I've read the reports. Fascinating."

"Why fascinating?" Ruthie asked.

"Because art thieves are not your run-of-the-mill burglars," she answered.

"What do you mean?" Ruthie asked.

"They're very particular about what they steal. Everyone knows what a television costs, but how about a Ming Dynasty vase? And not everyone knows how to distinguish a real one from a fake. Art thieves either have expertise or are working for someone who does."

"Are you worried?" Jack inquired.

"No. It's only the high-profile collectors who've been burgled. People know me as a book dealer, and my shop has a security system. Don't worry about me!"

As brunch came to an end, Ruthie popped up out of her chair. "Jack and I are going to the Art Institute and then to his house."

"You know, I still haven't seen the Thorne Rooms," Ruthie's mom said. "Remember, Ruthie, you promised to go through them with me one day. How about today?"

Ruthie, horrified by the idea, tried to keep a poker face. She was casting about for some excuse when Mrs. McVittie spoke up. "I'd like to join you as well, if I may. Dan, what about you? Why don't you come along?"

"I've got to grade papers," Mr. Stewart said with a shake of his head. "But you all go without me. You'll have fun!"

That was not the word Ruthie would have chosen.

A CHANCE MEETING?

IT TURNED OUT TO BE great that Mrs. McVittie went along with them, for a couple of reasons. First, Ruthie's mom insisted that they take a cab—something she rarely splurged on—which meant they would arrive at the museum much faster. Second, she gave Ruthie's mom someone to talk to instead of Ruthie. Ruthie sat squashed between her mother and Mrs. McVittie in the back while Jack sat up in front with the taxi driver, chatting with him all the way.

Heading up the stairs at the front of the museum, Jack filled her in on new trivia.

"Did you know they don't use knives and forks and stuff in Ethiopia when they eat?"

"What are you talking about?"

"They wrap their food in bread that's super thin, like your crepes."

"How do you know?" she asked, trying to hide her impatience.

"The cabdriver was from Ethiopia and he told me. You never know when you might need to know something like that."

When they got to the lobby, Ruthie said, "You guys go ahead; I'm gonna check my backpack." By the time she caught up with them, they had just finished the slow march down the main staircase.

"So this is it—the famous Thorne Rooms," Ruthie's mom said as they stood outside the entrance of Gallery 11, on the lower level of the museum. "I finally get to see what all the fuss is about!"

"I think you'll find that they are remarkable," Mrs. McVittie said.

Just inside the gallery a docent was giving a tour.

"Narcissa Thorne created the first set of European rooms, and then made the American rooms, mostly during the 1930s. Note that the rooms are numbered, E1 through E31 and A1 through A37. Some of the objects you'll see are antique miniatures that she collected from all over the world; others were made to her specifications by skilled artisans in her employ. The scale of the rooms is one inch to one foot, and all the materials are real—the furniture is real wood, the fireplace mantels real marble, the candlesticks real sterling, et cetera. The only fake things are those that would have been alive or might decay—for instance, flowers and food, and the dog lying in front of the fireplace in room E1."

Ruthie already knew all of this, inside and out. She gazed past the tour group to see the rooms set into the walls of the gallery, just at eye level. Sixty-eight little worlds, she thought, each so perfect and complete and— perhaps—filled with more secrets to discover. They beckoned to her from behind their viewing windows. Aside from the mystery of the key and its magic powers, the rooms themselves still felt new and exciting to her, the way they had when she'd seen them for the first time on the field trip three months ago. Goose bumps rose on her skin.

Ruthie did care about her mother's reaction, but right now she was driven to get to the bento box. She didn't wait for her mother and Mrs. McVittie, who wanted to look at the rooms one by one and in order. Ruthie had already turned the corner and was walking toward room E31, the Japanese room. Jack was right behind her.

Ruthie saw it first and gasped. There in the beautiful Japanese room sat Jack's bento box, in miniature. The box, which Jack had left sitting squarely on the table with the lid on, had been turned. And the lid was askew!

"I knew something was wrong!" Ruthie said in a hushed voice.

"I can't see if the letter is still in it or not." Jack tried to get a good angle. "Can you?"

"No," she answered.

"Maybe a maintenance person opened the glass front, like to do some dusting, and moved it accidentally. Maybe they didn't even see the letter."

"We've got to find out!" Ruthie insisted.

They were speaking very softly, not wanting the steady stream of viewers to overhear. Jack dropped his voice even further, saying, "I have the keys. Both of them." Jack was always prepared; he had the magic key and the key he had secretly copied months ago from Mr. Bell's museum keys, the one that opened the locked doors to the access corridors that ran behind all the rooms.

"But how can we do it? My mom's here!" At the thought of shrinking with her mother so close by, Ruthie felt her palms turn clammy. This wasn't something she'd planned on today.

At that moment her mother appeared around the corner.

"There you two are. Ruthie, you were right! Now I understand why you've been so bewitched by these rooms!" As her mother said the word *bewitched,* Mrs. McVittie smiled at Ruthie.

"Exactly! Magic! Right, Ruthie?" Mrs. McVittie said.

"Minerva tells me that she was about your age the first time she saw these rooms!" her mother went on. Ruthie tried to smile blankly as though she wasn't really interested in such ancient history. In fact, she knew far more than her mother about Mrs. McVittie and her magical visit in the Thorne Rooms so many years ago.

"Mrs. McVittie, let me show you something," Jack broke in, taking her arm and guiding her away from Ruthie and her mother.

"Why don't we go back to the beginning and you can show me the ones you like best?" Ruthie's mom suggested. That was the last thing Ruthie wanted to do at the moment. She only hoped that Jack would come back and interrupt them—soon.

They walked along, following the European rooms in order, her mother pointing out details that Ruthie knew so well: the candle stand from the castle room, E16, that Jack had used to fight off the cockroach; the ornately carved cabinet from E17 where she had discovered Mr. Bell's photo album; the cozy French bedroom, E22, where she and Jack had found the clothes from that time. She had to bite her tongue as she gazed into the rooms, reminding herself that her mother knew nothing about her adventures.

"This might be my favorite one yet: the French Revolutionary period!" her mother said. It was E24, Sophie's room. Ruthie tried not to overreact as she viewed the many-drawered desk she had sat at, with Sophie's journal right where she'd left it.

"The view through the windows is wonderful too." Her mother pointed to the painted dioramas that allowed glimpses of the outdoors. Ruthie spied eighteenth-century France from beyond the balcony curtains. Silently she relived the moment when she had first discovered the painted exterior was alive—when she and Jack had stepped out into that world and met Sophie. How strange it felt now to be standing outside looking in! Even without the necessity of retrieving the bento box and the letter, looking at the rooms like this made her realize that she wanted more adventures in them. There was so much exploring to do!

It couldn't have been more than ten minutes—although it felt much longer to Ruthie—before Jack and Mrs. McVittie reappeared alongside them. Mrs. McVittie held a linen handkerchief to her forehead.

"Minerva, are you feeling all right?" Ruthie's mom asked.

"Helen, would you take me to the ladies' room? I think I need to sit for a few minutes." Mrs. McVittie's voice sounded weak.

"Are you sure? I could take you home," she offered.

"No, no; it's just a little spell. There's a comfortable bench in there. I'll be fine if you keep me company until it passes," Mrs. McVittie assured her.

"She's totally faking," Jack explained as soon as the two women were out of the exhibition. "I told her everything. We have about fifteen, twenty minutes, max!"

Ruthie and Jack quickly backtracked to the little alcove that held the locked door to the European rooms' access corridor. The Thorne Rooms are displayed in Gallery 11 in two parts: the European rooms are installed along the perimeter walls, and the American rooms are in a U-shaped island in the middle of the gallery. Each has a corridor running behind the rooms that is off-limits to the public. To reach the Japanese room, which was the very last one, and check the bento box, Ruthie and Jack needed to get into the European corridor and follow it to the end.

"We can't unlock the door—there are too many people around," Jack said.

Ruthie looked about. The gallery was fairly crowded.

"Okay, this is how we'll do it," she suggested. "Since it only takes a second or two to shrink, you can stand in front of me and hand me the key right here. I'll shrink and squeeze under the door like we did before. No one will see because it'll be so fast and you can block me."

"Sounds good," Jack agreed.

"But wait—how will I get up to the room?" The rooms were about four feet off the ground and would be unreachable to a five-inch Ruthie. "I don't have time to build the staircase!" she worried aloud, remembering how long it had taken her to construct stairs out of the Thorne Rooms catalogues that were stored in the corridor.

"Ta-da!" Jack pulled out of his pocket the string-and-toothpick ladder that he'd made for their last adventure. "I thought it might come in handy! But you'll have to climb fast."

"And when I need to come out," Ruthie continued, "I'll look for you, okay?"

"Yeah. Just peek under first, to make sure no one's around. I might not be able to get here. If I'm not here, just leave the key there." He pointed to the floor near the door hinge. "I'll come back and get it right away." Ruthie couldn't hold the key without shrinking like Jack could—at least not so close to the corridor—so he would have to be the one to pick it up.

Ruthie thought that was a pretty good idea, and she was almost sure she could accomplish what needed to be done in the brief time she had. But she worried about the magic. After all, it had been a few months since she had held the key and had its magic act on her. What if it didn't work anymore?

Ruthie and Jack hovered near the alcove. Trying not to arouse suspicion, he slyly handed her the string ladder to put in her own pocket so it would shrink with her. He held the key in his own hand.

They waited. It seemed as though everyone in Chicago had chosen this day to come to the Thorne Rooms. Nearly three precious minutes passed before finally there was a break in the crowd, with no one looking in their direction. Jack stepped in front of Ruthie and swiftly pressed the key into her palm.

She gripped the key, her fingers wrapping tightly around it. *Please let it work,* Ruthie thought fleetingly. But the worries flew from her head in less than an instant. She had almost forgotten the sensations involved in the shrinking process. In a split second, a gentle breeze began to blow her hair. Her clothes caught up to her new size as she got smaller and smaller; she perceived what she thought must be the minute sound of threads crinkling. Her skin temporarily tightened ever so slightly and her muscles contracted as she shrank under the unstoppable force of the magic. Jack and the room melted into a weird expanding blur around her. When the process stopped, just a few seconds after the key had touched her palm, Ruthie stood five inches tall, and the now-enormous room came into focus. Tiny Ruthie scurried across the carpet—the loops of wool came nearly halfway up her shins—and scooted under the door.

The immense corridor was dark and dizzying. Ruthie, as small as a mouse in the vast space, crouched with her back against the giant door and looked up to the ledge that ran behind all the rooms. That was where she needed to be in order to have access to the rooms. She wanted to pause and regain her equilibrium, but she had to keep moving. She stood and let the key fall from her hand so she could go back to her full size, nearly losing her balance as she regrew. She felt her clothes tighten, then expand; her muscles tingled. The ledge appeared to descend to her height right in front of her!

Taking the rope ladder out of her pocket, she untangled it and secured it to the ledge with the little wire hooks Jack had fashioned. Then she picked up the key and let herself shrink again.

From her vantage point down on the floor, the ladder seemed higher than she remembered, and her head spun. But she had no other option, so she started the climb. She gripped the yarn, which was as thick as rope in her tiny hands. She could barely believe her weight was being supported

by toothpicks! *Don't look down,* she repeated to herself until she reached the top. She hurried along the ledge and around one turn, then another, until she reached the end.

Ruthie was out of breath by the time she reached the Japanese room. She hoped she could run in, grab the letter and the bento box and make her exit. Everything would be fine then, and she could stop worrying!

She approached the back of the room. Tiptoeing into the small hall to the left of the main room, Ruthie listened.

"Although Mrs. Thorne created the European rooms after her many travels there, she based the Chinese and the Japanese rooms on literary sources, having never visited Asia herself."

The museum docent must have stopped right in front of the room! Ruthie had no choice but to wait for her to leave. This could take forever. She worried about what would happen if her mom and Mrs. McVittie returned to the gallery before the tour moved on!

There was nothing Ruthie could do about this, so she went back out to the corridor. The last thing she wanted was to waste what little time she had. Luckily, one of her favorite places was just three rooms away. She couldn't resist; she decided she might as well slip in and explore for a couple of minutes rather than pace in the corridor.

E27 was a French library from the 1930s. It was hard for Ruthie to explain why she liked this particular room so much, but it had something to do with how open the space felt with its high ceiling. And of course it had a balcony! The room was entered by way of its roof garden—a luxury she would love to have in Chicago. She was pretty sure lots of rich people's apartments had them, but her family's didn't. The elegant garden was enclosed on one side by a tall limestone wall. A statue of a woman stood in front of it. There were small rectangular patches of grass and bushes trimmed into perfect globes. The voice of the docent was distant.

From the roof garden she peered into the room—no one was looking into it at the moment, so she entered. Because the room had two doors to the outside, a wonderful breeze blew through the space. And that breeze meant one thing: Paris was alive out there! The magic was working!

Ruthie scanned the room. The furniture was covered in rich silks and satins. One wall was decorated with a tapestry of a city scene in geometric shapes, like a painting by Picasso. She walked over to touch the surface. Her hand felt the small stitches, and she marveled at how incredibly tiny they must have been to the full-sized hand that made them.

Voices grew louder as visitors approached the viewing window, and Ruthie ducked behind an upholstered chair in the corner. She crouched there while two sets of people passed by, exclaiming about catching a glimpse of the Eiffel Tower through the balcony door.

When there was a lull in the crowd Ruthie ran across the room to absorb the sunshine of 1930s Paris. The balcony—which was separate from the rooftop garden—was big enough for a table and chairs. The glass-topped table was set with two golden water goblets and shiny green plates. Cheery zinnias bloomed from two orange planters. Out of sight to museum visitors, a spiral staircase wound down to a small, enclosed courtyard between the building and the street. Ruthie had never seen a staircase like this on the outside of a building. Standing in a spot where she was sure no viewers could spy her, she looked out over a spectacular panorama of a wide boulevard and the Eiffel Tower beyond. She could see lots of people down in the street and a bustling city park. In fact, there seemed to be some sort of festival going on, with flags from different countries waving and music competing with the sounds of laughter and shouting.

Ruthie inhaled deeply one more time before leaving the balcony. She was so tempted to walk down that spiral staircase and into Paris! But her five minutes were up—the gallery tour must have moved on by now. Not letting herself forget the urgent errand she was on, she left the room and raced back to E31.

She heard the muffled voices of people in the exhibition but could tell that the docent was no longer speaking right in front of E31. Two voices in particular, though, were becoming more distinct: Jack's and the voice of a woman, not her mother or Mrs. McVittie. She peeked around the corner, into the room, and through the viewing window. She saw Jack's head in profile as he spoke.

"What are you sketching?" Ruthie heard Jack ask. She couldn't see whom he was talking to, but she listened carefully.

"This Chinese room. I'm studying all of the rooms," a woman's voice answered. "What do you think?"

"Pretty good," Jack said approvingly. "You really got the details."

The Chinese room was right next to the Japanese room. Ruthie realized Jack was keeping this woman away from the window by talking about her drawing. This way, he blocked anyone else from looking into the room while Ruthie got the job done.

Ruthie crept into the room, walked over to the low lacquered table and opened the bento box. The letter was still there, folded just as they'd left it. She breathed a sigh of relief and put it in her pocket. Then she let herself take one more look into the Zen garden adjoining the room on the right. Something felt wrong. She stepped in. Surprisingly, the garden seemed extremely quiet, with no rustling of trees or sounds of birds chirping; the air felt stale. The plants looked fake, and she could even see some chipped paint in the corner of the sky.

Ruthie worried that the magic was weakening, that perhaps standing on that Parisian balcony had used too much power. Or maybe it was simply that this room was not a portal to the past like the other rooms. Her curiosity ballooned inside her, but exploring would have to wait. Her mother and Mrs. McVittie would return from the restroom any minute. It had been at least ten minutes since she climbed the ladder; she had to hustle.

Ruthie turned to leave the garden, but as soon as she did, she caught sight of the blond head of the woman who was talking to Jack. Ruthie jumped back, unsure whether she had been seen. Finally she heard Jack ask which room was the woman's favorite, and they moved away. Ruthie scrambled across the tatami floor mats, swiftly picking up the bento box on her way to the small hall and then back out to the corridor.

She ran as fast as she could along the narrow ledge. Once at the ladder, she decided it would be too difficult— not to mention slow—to climb down the ladder while holding the bento box. Clutching it, she leapt off the ledge, letting the key fall to the floor. Ruthie and the key landed in tandem, now full-sized. She detached the ladder from the ledge. Then she picked up the key and shrank again.

Ruthie reached the door and looked under; no one was there. She shoved the tiny bento box under the door (it would be too big to carry around in her pocket at full size, and her mother would most certainly ask where it had come from) and then squeezed under just far enough to look about the gallery. Jack was nowhere in sight. She watched as shoes, their soles as thick as mattresses, passed by in a steady stream. It seemed like a long wait until she was able to come all the way out and place the key at the base of the door for Jack to retrieve. In seconds she was big again. She picked up the miniature bento box and slipped it into her pocket; it looked like the bump from a pot of lip gloss.

Ruthie was certain her adventure would somehow show on her face. She found Jack still talking to the striking woman who was sketching the rooms. The woman was tall and thin, with perfect posture, and her very light hair was pulled back tightly. With her designer glasses and pointy-toed shoes she looked like a model from a fashion magazine. Ruthie had hoped to find Jack alone; she couldn't stop thinking about the key sitting on the floor of the alcove. She wanted it back in Jack's pocket as fast as possible.

"There you are," Jack said. "This is Dora. She's studying the Thorne Rooms. This is my friend Ruthie." Ruthie gave him an intense look, which he understood. "I'll be right back." He turned and headed back to recover the key.

"Nice to meet you." Dora smiled at Ruthie. "Jack tells me the two of you wrote a report for school about the Thorne Rooms."

"I'm kinda obsessed with them," Ruthie admitted.

"Join the club!" Dora laughed.

"Your drawings are beautiful," Ruthie admired.

"I've been working on them for a few weeks." Dora turned several pages so that Ruthie could take a look. The last was the unfinished sketch of the Chinese room. The intricately carved wood screens that divided the room were finely penciled. Dora had even captured the subtle expression on the face of the ancestor portrait that hung on the back wall. "What do you think?"

"They're really good," Ruthie said, feeling like her praise was not strong enough. The drawings were exceptional.

"Thank you," Dora answered.

"Are you an artist?" Ruthie asked.

"No. I'm an interior decorator—I'm getting a master's degree in design from the School of the Art Institute, and I'm using the Thorne Rooms as part of my research on historic interiors."

"That's what Mrs. Thorne wanted people to do." Ruthie remembered what she'd learned in the archives.

"Exactly," Dora agreed.

Ruthie continued to browse through the perfectly rendered sketches.

"Here you are." Ruthie looked up and saw her mother and Mrs. McVittie approaching them. "Where's Jack?" her mother asked.

"Right here," Jack said, coming around the corner from the other direction. He gave Ruthie a quick look, his hand subtly patting his pocket, meaning he had the key safely tucked away. No one but Ruthie noticed.

"Look, Mom." Ruthie held up Dora's sketchbook for her mother and Mrs. McVittie to see.

Dora offered her hand in greeting. "Dora Pommeroy. Pleased to meet you."

"Helen Stewart," Ruthie's mom replied, shaking hands. "And this is Minerva McVittie."

Mrs. McVittie also held out her hand. "Have we met before?"

"I don't think so," Dora answered.

"I'm sure we have. I never forget a face," Mrs. McVittie pressed.

Ruthie decided to interrupt before Mrs. McVittie started talking about all the possible places they might have met. Grown-ups could go on forever about that.

"I wish I could draw like that," Ruthie said aloud.

"Anyone can learn to draw," Dora said. "Have you ever had lessons?"

"Just art class in school. I got an A, but I'm not that good, really," Ruthie confessed. "Jack's better."

"My mom's an artist. I have to be good," Jack explained.

"What did you say your last name is? Tucker, right?" Dora asked.

"Yep, that's right," Jack confirmed.

"Is your mother Lydia Tucker, the painter?"

"Yeah. Have you heard of her?" Jack was always surprised when anyone had heard of his mother. Ruthie thought he should be used to it by now.

"I've seen her work. Her trompe l'oeil murals are amazing," Dora enthused.

"Thanks, I guess," Jack responded awkwardly. "Could you give Ruthie lessons?"

"I do give private lessons occasionally," she responded.

"Please, Mom," Ruthie implored. "I would love to learn how to draw these rooms!"

"Let's think about it. Do you have a card, Ms. Pommeroy?" her mom asked.

Dora rummaged through her bag, pulled out a card, and handed it to Ruthie's mom. "Why don't you send me an email?"

Ruthie looked at the card in her mother's hand. It read *Pandora Pommeroy Interiors*.

3

AN ANONYMOUS REPLY

"**D**ID YOU GET THE LETTER? And I saw my bento box isn't in the room anymore; where is it?" Jack asked when all three adults were safely a few paces away.

"The letter's in my pocket. And your bento box is here." She reached into her front pocket and pulled out the miniature box. "Here, you take it. I couldn't bring it out at full size because I didn't have anywhere to put it."

Jack stashed it in one of the multiple large pockets of his cargo pants, snapping the pocket flap closed.

They spent another half hour in the rooms. After reclaiming her backpack from the coat check, Ruthie turned to her mother and said, "I'm going to Jack's house to do homework. Okay, Mom?"

Ruthie was walking just behind Jack as they passed through the Michigan Avenue doors, and she noticed his side pocket suddenly expand like a bag of microwave popcorn.

Startled, he turned around briefly to check if Ruthie's mom or anyone else had seen. Ruthie immediately realized what was happening: the bento box had regained its full size, unsnapping the closure of Jack's pocket and bursting its seams. Fortunately, her mother was standing on his other side.

Mrs. McVittie, who was next to Ruthie, noticed the strange phenomenon and quickly grabbed Ruthie's mom's arm. "Helen, I seem to be having another spell. Do you mind seeing me home?"

She could win an Academy Award, Ruthie thought gratefully.

"Of course, Minerva." Ruthie's mom focused her full attention on her friend, helping her down the front steps. Jack and Ruthie stayed back a few feet.

"That was close," Jack said in a low voice.

"I should have figured this would happen! I just didn't think," Ruthie said as she dragged Jack behind one of the big bronze lions that stood halfway up the steps. "It's exactly like what happened to us when we spent the night in the museum. Remember when we left the corridor to run to the restrooms? We were full-sized before we got there!"

Jack took the box out of his now-ripped pocket.

"So all the stuff in the rooms that started off full-sized will stay small only in or near the rooms," Ruthie went on.

"Must be," Jack agreed. He handed Ruthie the bento box, and she put it in her backpack. "And remember when we were in A1 from the time of the Salem witch trials—Thomas Wilcox's room?"

"The *Mayflower* model!" Ruthie exclaimed.

"The archive papers we read said it came from an antiques dealer, right? Not a miniatures dealer; that's how we knew Thomas' *Mayflower* was made full-sized." Then Jack added, "I wonder how many objects are magically shrunk in the rooms."

With Ruthie's mom and Mrs. McVittie on their way home in a cab, Ruthie and Jack hopped on the bus to Jack's house. They walked down the aisle and found two empty seats at the back. "Oh, I almost forgot," Ruthie said as the bus started forward. "While I was waiting for that tour group to move I looked in another room."

"Which one?"

"E27—it's a room from Paris in 1937. It was alive, Jack. Just like Sophie's room and Thomas'."

"Cool. Are you sure?"

"Positive. It has a balcony, and I could see people in the streets. It looked like some kind of fair was happening. I want to go back."

"We should probably learn some French, huh?" Jack suggested.

"My mom would be thrilled," Ruthie said. Her mom taught French at Oakton and was always trying to get Ruthie to study it.

"Let's see the letter," Jack said.

Ruthie took the letter out of her back pocket and unfolded it. She and Jack looked at it and then at each other in disbelief.

Jack's handwritten note, which they had both signed, read:

To whom it may concern,
    Ruthie Stewart and Jack Tucker, sixth-grade students in Chicago, visited these rooms by way of a magic key. We think the magic came from Christina of Milan (see room E1). If you are reading this, it means you are experiencing the magic too. Others have done this before us. Good luck!

At the bottom of their note someone had written:

If this is not a joke, leave another note.

The handwriting had an odd appearance.

"It looks like someone tried to write really small, doesn't it?" Ruthie observed.

"Yeah—like someone used a full-sized pencil. See—the thickness of the lines is all wrong," Jack said. "We could write an answer, saying it was a joke."

"That won't totally solve the problem. Whoever it is will still know we snuck into the rooms." They both kept looking at the note as though answers would appear on the page. People walking in the aisle jostled them as the bus made its stops. "But they don't know about the shrinking. They could think we just wrote really tiny and somehow put the note in from the front."

"I think we need to find out who wrote it," Jack said.

"That's going to be hard. And whoever wrote this already knows who we are! Our names are in it."

Ruthie felt a sudden sensation of paranoia. She looked at the people around her on the bus and the hundreds of people they were passing on the street. Any one of them could be the person who wrote the anonymous note. She folded the letter and clutched it close.

"I wonder how long it's been there?" Jack asked.

"It could be a trap," Ruthie said. "You know, someone at the museum who wants to know how we got the note in there. Or it could be someone just like us, someone who wants answers."

Concentrating on their homework proved extremely difficult; as soon as they'd answered the last question in the history book, Jack slapped it closed.

"Okay. List time. We need to make a list of all the facts we know about the magic."

Ruthie took a small spiral-bound notebook from her backpack. She turned to a fresh page, ready to write.

In about ten minutes they had a pretty thorough list:

1. The magic comes from the key that Christina, Duchess of Milan, had made for her in the sixteenth century.

2. The shrinking can happen only when a female is holding the key in her hand.

3. The shrinking happens only within a certain distance from the rooms. The bigger the object (like a human), the smaller the distance away from the rooms before you regrow. Small objects, like a bento box, can go pretty far before regrowing (near the doors of the museum, for instance).

4. The unshrinking also happens when a shrunk female lets go of the key somewhere in the corridor or in the area nearby.

5. Once small, the female must keep the key with her, like in a pocket, to stay small, except if she is in the rooms (or outside in the past worlds).

6. A male can shrink if he is holding hands with the shrinking female.

7. Some of the rooms are "alive"—we think these rooms are portals to the past.

8. The time of day in the past worlds is determined by the painted worlds outside the rooms, and the "clock" starts ticking when a person from now enters the past (we think). Once we are in the outside worlds, the time seems to pass just like normal. We have no idea how this part of the magic works.

9. We don't know if Mrs. Thorne or her craftsmen knew about this, but we think maybe they did.

10. Stuff from the past (like the arrows that were shot into the window of the French castle room) disappears if it ends up in the rooms. But the antiques that Mrs. Thorne put in the rooms on purpose stay there.

"Anything else?" Ruthie asked.

"I'm sure we'll think of more." Jack stretched.

"We should probably make a list of who could have written the message," Ruthie suggested.

"Mr. Bell," Jack stated matter-of-factly.

"You really think so?" Ruthie was skeptical.

"Maybe. He has access to the rooms."

"*Had* access," Ruthie corrected him. Since Ruthie and Jack had discovered his lost work, Mr. Bell had retired from his guard job. For the past month he had been working solely as an artist.

"Yeah, but he could've put the note in there right before he left," Jack said.

"He knows us. Don't you think he would have said something directly to us?"

"Maybe, maybe not. It's pretty unbelievable, after all."

"How about the archive curator, the one who helped us on the report?"

Jack nodded, then added, "Any of the other guards or maintenance people."

Then something occurred to Ruthie. "Jack, remember what Mr. Bell's daughter said at the opening last night?"

"Caroline Bell? About what?"

"About how her backpack was lost. She said the three of us have more to talk about. Remember, you elbowed me. I think we should try to meet with her."

"And just ask her if she knows anything about the note?"

"No, not about the note exactly. But to see if maybe we can trust her. To see if she wants to know anything more about her memories and the rooms. Maybe she can help us."

"Okay. Put her down."

As she wrote the name, Ruthie realized something else. "Maybe whoever put the note in the box will notice that it's gone now and come looking for us."

"You're right," Jack agreed soberly. "We'd better put it back. Tuesday—it's a half day of school."

They sat on the floor of his room, looking from the letter to the list and back again, quietly mulling the situation. The silence was broken by the sound of a key opening the loft door.

"Hello," Lydia called into the big space.

"Hi, Mom." Jack got up. "We're here."

Jack and Ruthie went into the kitchen area.

"Hello, Ruthie." Lydia had just put down a bag of groceries and was looking through the mail. She smiled at Jack. "Yesterday's mail. We forgot to bring it up," she said. "And today's paper. I hear we're in the Arts section." She opened the paper on the kitchen table and thumbed through to find their pictures. "Ah, here we are. Hey, you two look pretty good! . . . Oh boy." Her tone changed as she skimmed another article. "I was wondering if this would make the papers. I've been hearing about this from some of my friends. An art thief!"

"My family saw that too," Ruthie said.

"What else do you know, Mom?"

"Not much more than what it says here in the article. Word is it's been going on for several weeks; there aren't any clues." Lydia turned her attention to opening the mail. "What have you two been up to today?"

"We took my mom to see the Thorne Rooms," Ruthie said.

"Yeah, and I met someone who's maybe going to give Ruthie drawing lessons," Jack added.

"Really? Who?

"Dora Pommeroy. She's an interior designer," Ruthie answered.

"She said she'd heard of you, Mom."

"I've met her a few times. She's decorated homes of some people who've bought my paintings; she has a great reputation. I don't know her well, though." Lydia showed Jack a card that had come in the mail. "Look at this. It's an invitation to a gala at the Art Institute—and I can bring a guest."

"Do you have to dress up?" Jack asked with an obvious lack of enthusiasm.

"Yes. Gala means you dress up," she answered. "I bet I could bring you both."

"I'd love to!" Ruthie looked at Jack, wondering why he didn't appear to understand the opportunity this might present—being in the museum after it was closed! Now Ruthie had two things to look forward to: drawing lessons and an evening at the museum!

"So my first drawing lesson is going to be on Saturday. My mom got an email from Dora last night," Ruthie told Jack. It was Tuesday afternoon, chilly but clear and sunny. She and Jack sped two steps at a time up to the front doors of the museum. "We're going to meet here and she's going to bring the supplies I need."

Jack didn't seem to be paying attention. "Do you have money to check your backpack?" he asked.

"Yep." She retrieved a dollar out of her pocket. They set their backpacks down on a bench just inside the entrance. "And I brought this." She pulled a canvas messenger-type bag out of her backpack. "I can bring this into the museum. We can carry the bento box in it."

"Good thinking." He slipped the bento box out of his backpack and lifted the lid to show Ruthie the letter safe inside. "Here, take this too." He handed her the tiny rolled-up string ladder.

"Where's the key?" Ruthie asked.

Jack patted the pocket of his sweatshirt jacket. The line for the coat check was long but moved fast.

"It's so crowded today," Ruthie commented as they bounded down the marble staircase. Unfortunately, not every school had a half day, and the museum seemed to be bursting with school groups on field trips.

They hovered around the alcove, not looking at any of the rooms. The more Ruthie tried to act normal, the more she felt certain she seemed guilty of something. A guard came by and gave them a long glance.

"This is torture," Ruthie whispered.

"Just look at the rooms," Jack said. They walked across the space, back to the wall of European rooms, and stood in front of room E6, an English library from the early 1700s. The library was directly next to the alcove.

"That's odd," Ruthie said. "Something's missing."

"What do you mean?" Jack asked.

"See the smallish globe on the desk there?"

"Yeah. What about it?"

"There should be two of them. One on each side of the desk," Ruthie said.

"Are you sure?"

"Positive. I know one's missing because I thought it was weird to have two globes in the first place," she explained.

"Is it somewhere else in the room?"

Ruthie and Jack spent a minute looking.

"No. It's definitely gone," said Ruthie. "I'll show you later in the cata—"

"Quick!" Jack grabbed Ruthie and pulled her to the alcove. They had three or four seconds with no one nearby. He slammed the key into Ruthie's hand and she closed her fist around it. In the blink of an eye, Ruthie's ponytail was swinging in the breeze that surrounded them, the alcove enlarging into a cavernous space.

They fell to their hands and knees on the giant carpet loops and rolled under the door. In the corridor, Jack jumped up and down like a tiny prizefighter.

"It worked! I almost forgot how cool this is!"

"Yeah, but we've got to get big again to set up the ladder," Ruthie reminded him.

"You can do it without me. Let me stay small and you can lift me up."

"Oh, all right," Ruthie said, feeling like his chauffeur.

She dropped the key and returned to full size. Jack lifted the key, which was now almost as large as him, staggering under its weight.

"If I carry you while you've got the key, you're gonna have to make sure it doesn't touch me!" Ruthie cautioned. "I don't want to shrink while I'm holding you!"

Jack held the key in front of him with his hands outstretched. He looked like an old-fashioned doll whose arms didn't bend. Ruthie carefully picked him up between her thumb and index finger, holding him at the waist, his legs dangling.

"Go fast," Jack's tiny voice ordered. "I don't think I can hold the key very long."

Ruthie jogged down the dark corridor, Jack bouncing along. At E31 Ruthie placed him on the ledge.

"Man, that was heavy!" Jack let the key fall from his hands.

Ruthie secured the ladder to the ledge, then picked up the key and shrank along with the canvas bag, the bento box, and the letter. Wishing she could be in Jack's place on the ledge, she started the long climb.

"There are so many people out there right now," Jack said as Ruthie arrived on the ledge. "I just checked."

"Here." She handed him the bento box. "You can put it back." Ruthie was glad to rest after the long climb. She sat down and watched as Jack took the box and made his way through the opening in the framework, which led to the side room where he would wait for a break in the crowd.

"That was close," Jack said when he reappeared. "Someone almost saw me, and I had to dive into the garden. It's weird," he added. "It feels different in there since the last time. The garden was real, alive, before. Now it's fake."

"I'm pretty sure it wasn't alive when I went in there on Sunday. I noticed that right away."

"I wonder why it's not."

"All I know is that E27 is most definitely magic," Ruthie responded. "Or at least it was on Sunday. Let's go."

Ruthie and Jack ran along the ledge, past the Chinese interior and a German sitting room. She led Jack to the opening for room E27. Stepping into the beautiful rooftop garden, the two instantly felt what Ruthie had experienced before—it was alive!

"Wow. This is pretty awesome!" Jack looked off into the distance through a window in the high wall that enclosed the garden.

"Jack, watch out!" Ruthie ordered. "People can see you from there." It was true. Room E27 had two doorways—one leading out to the roof garden, and the other to a balcony. Viewers from the museum could look through either door and see not only the long vistas of Paris but Jack as well. He swung around and ducked out of the way at the very moment a head came into view.

Ruthie joined him in the safe spot. "Isn't it fantastic?"

"What year did you say it was?" Jack asked.

"The catalogue said 1937—the year of some kind of big fair." She peeked around the corner. "Come on!"

Jack followed her into the room. "It's so different from Sophie's room." He admired the high ceilings and simple, geometric lines.

"We can't stay here—the museum is too crowded. Let's

go out to the balcony." Ruthie led him out of the room, through the door on the right.

Out there, where no viewers could see them, they heard the sounds of the street mixed with music and voices, just as Ruthie had during her brief first visit. She looked at Jack. "Want to explore?"

"Yes!" he answered.

· · · 4 · · ·
LOUISA

THEY MADE THEIR WAY DOWN and around—six times—
on the outdoor spiral staircase. At the bottom they
found themselves in a formal garden courtyard, much like
the one on the rooftop. Several beautiful white stone
sculptures stood next to precisely trimmed bushes.
Aromatic roses bloomed in four squared-off sections with
paths in between, and an elaborately decorated wrought-
iron gate led to the street. Jack opened it and stuck his
head out to check what was happening on the sidewalk.

Ruthie noticed a key hanging from a nail on the garden
wall. She put it in one of her pockets to make sure they
wouldn't get locked out, and then joined Jack on the sidewalk. The weighty iron gate clanged shut behind them.

So this is Paris in 1937, Ruthie thought, wide-eyed, as
she looked all around. White stone buildings—uniformly
about six stories tall—faced the wide boulevard. Sycamore

trees trimmed into perfect rectangles lined the streets. Ruthie thought they looked like giant leafy ice cream bars on sticks. A few blocks off, the Eiffel Tower rose high above all the other buildings. A well-dressed woman walked by carrying in a little basket the smallest dog Ruthie had ever seen.

Another woman passed them pulling a wheeled shopping cart, a baguette sticking out from the top. Except for the hairdos and clothes and the shapes of the cars, it looked just like the pictures in her mother's books. The women all wore dresses or skirts and high heels and had neatly waved hair. Most of the men were in suits and leather shoes—no blue jeans or sneakers in sight. The sidewalks were dotted with cafés on every corner, filled with people, many of them smoking cigarettes, which made Ruthie aware of all the other scents around her; strong coffee, car exhaust, perfumes. The sun shone mid-day bright.

"What month do you think it is?" Jack asked.

"Early summer?" Ruthie saw that the leaves on the trees still looked light green and fresh. They walked down the street, getting a few stares but mostly being ignored. They noted the street signs so they would be sure not to get lost as they wandered.

When Ruthie and Jack had met Sophie in Paris in the eighteenth century, the Eiffel Tower hadn't been built yet. But now, turning a corner, they found themselves standing at the top of a long, open pedestrian space spreading out in front of them. The beautiful metalwork tower stood at the far end. What must have been thousands of people filled their view.

"I can't believe we're really here!"

"Me neither!" Jack agreed.

Ruthie mentally compared the scene to the pictures in her mother's books. She recognized this view of the city as the Jardins du Trocadéro. A long, rectangular fountain ran down the center of the gardens, its jets spraying water dramatically into the air. The ground sloped to the Seine River and a bridge that people walked across to the Eiffel Tower. That was all the same as in the books. However, the park was lined with small buildings of different styles, with flags of various countries waving near the doors or from the rooftops. Ruthie couldn't be absolutely certain, but she didn't remember any of these buildings from the books. Two of these structures at the end of the park stood out from the rest; they were larger and faced each other.

"Let's walk down there," she suggested.

Everyone seemed interested in this pair of unusual buildings on either side of the wide promenade. When Ruthie and Jack neared the end they stopped to look at them.

"Whoa." Ruthie gazed up at a tall, tower-like structure. It was all white stone and designed with straight vertical lines, which made it seem even taller. A huge sculpture of an eagle perched on the top, its lifelike eyes intense and focused on the park below. Flagpoles on the ground

surrounded the structure. On each pole they saw the flag of Nazi Germany. Even though the sun was shining, Ruthie felt a chill.

"What do you know about this time in history—1937?" Ruthie asked, once again glad that Jack was such a history buff.

"It was before the start of World War Two, but just barely, I think. Germany was getting pretty powerful— that's probably why this is the tallest of all these buildings." He turned to look directly across at the other side of the promenade. "Look at that one."

Ruthie pivoted and saw the second-tallest structure. It was made of gray stone and had two huge statues—a man and a woman—on the top of it. The figures seemed to be striding forward with large steps and together held something above their heads.

"Do you know what they're holding?" Ruthie asked.

"That's the hammer and sickle from the Soviet flag. See, there's the flag." Jack pointed to two red flags on flagpoles next to the door of the structure. "From when Russia was called the Soviet Union."

"This one gives me the creeps too," she responded. "These two buildings look like they're competing with each other."

"That would make sense. Germany and the Soviet Union were enemies in World War Two."

She looked up at the two menacing towers; a wave of fear ran through her, and she unconsciously took a step back. But as she did so, she felt her foot step on something before it hit the ground—something soft that gave a little yelp. Ruthie caught herself and turned fast, nearly tripping. The yelp had come from a little dachshund.

"Frieda!" the girl at the other end of the leash said. "Sitz!" The obedient dog sat.

"I'm so sorry," Ruthie apologized.

"No, I am sorry. She shouldn't be underfoot!"

"She's really cute!" Ruthie reached down to stroke the little dog.

"Are you from America?" the girl asked.

"Yes," Jack answered. "My name's Jack, and this is Ruthie."

"I am Louisa." She looked to be about the same age as them. She wore a cotton print dress with a blue cardigan sweater. Only the top button was buttoned, which seemed to be the style on lots of women out walking. Her dark hair was pulled back from her face with two fancy clips. "I could tell from your accent—and your clothes." Ruthie and Jack both wore blue jeans and sneakers. Jack had the image of Sue the dinosaur from the Field Museum on his T-shirt, her toothy *T. rex* smile poking out from under his sweatshirt jacket. Ruthie wore a blue sweatshirt with the Oakton logo printed on it. "Does everyone dress like this in America these days?"

"In Chicago," Jack answered. "That's where we're from."

"I have heard there are gangsters there!" Louisa said.

Ruthie was about to answer no, but Jack answered first.

"It's true. Al Capone." Ruthie had no idea what Jack was talking about, so she kept quiet. "The FBI has caught most of them, though. It's pretty safe now."

"What are you doing in Paris?" Louisa asked.

Again Jack answered quickly. "Our dad is here on business. It's our second time in Paris."

At least that's half true, Ruthie thought.

"What about you?" Ruthie asked. She had noticed right away that this girl's perfect English had an accent that didn't sound French. And she was pretty sure that when the girl had told her dog to sit, she hadn't said it in French.

"I am German. My family came to Paris a few months ago." She changed the subject. "What do you think of the exposition?"

"We don't know much about it. What's it all about?"

Frieda whimpered and tugged on the leash, so they all started walking alongside the fountain as Louisa talked.

"This is the Exposition Universelle. The organizers say it is meant to celebrate progress and the future. Every country has a pavilion." She gestured to the structures that lined the park. "Each pavilion shows what is new in that country."

"Oh, I get it," Ruthie said. "It's a World's Fair." Her father had told her about some famous buildings in Chicago built for one of those fairs a long time ago. The three of them walked up and down the Jardins du Trocadéro; they noted the pavilions of Poland, Finland, and Spain (Louisa helped them recognize the names with their foreign spellings). These buildings sat lower and welcomed visitors, unlike the looming structures from Germany and the Soviet Union, which seemed to command, *Stay out!*

Louisa asked all kinds of questions about Chicago, and told Ruthie and Jack a lot about Paris and Berlin and the people of the two cities.

"The secret is," she began, "sometimes I feel rather out of place here. Parisians are so different from Berliners."

"You'd fit in at our school," Jack said. "Everyone is pretty different."

"What do you mean?" she asked.

"Lots of our classmates' families come from somewhere else. Even our teacher, Ms. Biddle, grew up outside of the States—her mom's Nigerian and her dad's from England," Jack explained.

"That sounds fun," Louisa said.

"Do you go to school here?" Ruthie asked.

"No, since it is temporary. My brother and I have a tutor for lessons, though." Then she turned toward the river and pointed. "The United States pavilion is down by the Seine over there."

"Let's go see it," Ruthie suggested.

They walked to the bridge that crossed the Seine, seeing the tourist boats pass under. The sunlight hit the waves created by them, glints bouncing off the white foam. On the other side, they turned to the right, passing the pavilions of Great Britain, Sweden, and Czechoslovakia. The

U.S. pavilion was a symmetrical building with a windowed tower in the middle that was much taller than the rest of the building. A single U.S. flag waved on top. It looked like a typical office building. There was a long line of people waiting to go inside, and Ruthie and Jack knew they didn't have time for that.

"You know what I've always wanted to do?" Jack suddenly said. "Stand right under the Eiffel Tower."

"Now's your chance!" Ruthie responded. They backtracked to the tower.

"This is awesome!" Jack said as he found the spot directly under the center of the tower. "If you look long enough, it seems like it's spinning!"

The four massive legs sloped up around them and the rays of the sun poked through the metal lattice. It seemed so much bigger than either of them had expected.

"It is beautiful, no?" Louisa offered.

"It really is," Ruthie agreed. Then she heard a man's voice that seemed to be directed at them, even though she couldn't make out anything he was saying. Ruthie saw that a vendor a few feet away was calling to them and laughing a bit. "Is he saying something to us?" she asked Louisa.

"Uh, well, yes," Louisa answered tentatively.

"What's he saying?"

"He is asking if you are American. He says you are dressed like them," Louisa translated.

Ruthie felt a little insulted, but Jack just laughed. "He's got that right. Hey, what's he selling?"

The vendor smiled at them, now that he had their attention, and they decided to look at his wares. They saw postcards of Paris and the exposition, along with a wide variety of souvenirs.

"Look at this." Jack pointed to a small red model airplane. It had a single propeller and was the type that would have been big enough for only a few passengers. "It looks familiar."

"Bonjour, mes amis américains!" the man said in a big, friendly voice.

Louisa automatically translated for him. "He said, 'Hello, my American friends.'"

"Vous aimez? You like?" He picked up the toy plane and handed it to Jack.

"Yes," Jack replied. *"Oui."*

"C'est l'avion d'Amelia, la belle aviatrice américaine."

Jack and Ruthie looked toward Louisa.

"He said, 'It is the plane of Amelia, the beautiful American aviator.'"

"That's where I've seen it before—it's Amelia Earhart's Vega!"

"Pour les jeunes américains, un cadeau!"

"He said, 'For the young Americans, a gift.' He wants to give you this plane!"

Jack's eyes lit up. Ruthie looked at him. "We can't, Jack."

"Sure we can. He wants to give it to us!"

"Je vous en prie." The man was pushing the plane into Jack's hand. *"J'insiste."*

"'Please,' he said. He insists," Louisa translated.

"What's the big deal?" Jack said to Ruthie.

"Never mind." Ruthie turned to the vendor. *"Merci beaucoup."*

Even Jack knew what that meant, and he repeated the phrase.

"*Vive* Amelia Earhart!" the man said, and then handed Ruthie two small flags, one French and one American. She smiled at him and waved the two flags.

Louisa explained, "The French like Americans—except the way they dress!"

Jack looked at the model plane in his hands. It was made of metal and hand-painted with fine details. "This is outstanding."

"You know, we'd better start heading back," Ruthie said.

"So must I," Louisa echoed. "My mother will worry."

"Do you live near here?" Jack asked as they crossed the bridge.

"Yes. Just over there." She pointed across the park to a row of beautiful buildings. "It is very nice. But I miss my home in Berlin. And my school. And my friends."

"Where did you learn such good English?" Ruthie asked.

"It is taught in my school in Berlin. But I also have American relatives. They don't speak any German at all, so we must speak in English when they come to visit."

"Your English is perfect," Jack admired.

"Thank you very much!" She beamed at the compliment.

"How long will your family be staying in Paris?" Ruthie wanted to know.

"Until we can go back to Berlin." Louisa's voice sounded sad.

"What do you mean?" Ruthie asked.

"We can't go home now. Because of them," she said, pointing over her shoulder to the big Nazi tower across the way.

"The Nazis?" Jack asked.

"Yes; they are running the government. My father can't work in Germany right now."

Of course Ruthie knew a little bit about what had happened in Germany under the Nazis, but now she wished she knew more. "What does your father do?" Ruthie asked.

"He is a surgeon. They took away his license because we are Jewish. But my father says it will get sorted out and we will go back soon." Louisa seemed uncomfortable with the subject. "I really must be going now. Will you come to the Jardins du Trocadéro again?"

Ruthie was about to answer no, but Jack was faster.

"Oh, sure. We'll probably see you again," he answered.

"If you don't see me with Frieda, come to my house. Number seven, rue Le Tasse. Second from the end. You will see the name Meyer on the doorbell. Just ring." She smiled at them. "I mustn't be late. *À bientôt,* Ruthie and Jack."

Ruthie smiled back, knowing what she had said. *"À bientôt!"*

Louisa ran off with Frieda, whose long ears flopped while her short legs moved so fast it appeared she had eight instead of four.

"She's nice," Ruthie said as soon as Louisa was out of earshot.

"We'd better go back—it's getting late."

As they left the Jardins du Trocadéro, they passed by a newsstand that they hadn't noticed before. There were several magazines and newspapers. The one on the biggest pile had the words *Le Temps* written across the top.

"Hey, look," Jack said, pointing to the date on it. Ruthie read *18 juin 1937.*

"Juin is June," Ruthie declared.

"Wow. That's just a little over seventy years ago," Jack said. He turned to Ruthie. "Amelia Earhart is flying around the world right now! She took off at the beginning of June in 1937!"

"Wow. But didn't she . . . she didn't make it, did she?"

"Exactly," Jack said. "It's kinda amazing that we're the only people on the planet right now who know that. In just a few weeks she'll be declared missing. . . ." His voice trailed off and he gazed at the little red plane. "I wonder . . ."

"If we could do anything to save her?" Ruthie had been

thinking the same thing. "She's one of the most famous people of the century; we'd be changing history!"

"We could go to the embassy, or call the newspaper."

"What would we say to convince them? 'You've got to stop Amelia Earhart—her plane is going to crash'? Do you think anyone would believe us?"

"Not a chance," Jack conceded. "Man, that's sad."

Ruthie wrapped her brain around this dilemma. "Amelia Earhart knew the risk she was taking. She chose the danger."

"I guess she's sort of like the astronauts."

"Right. If she accepted the odds, then probably we should too." This made sense to Ruthie, but she hated that she couldn't do anything about it. They arrived at the spiral staircase and began the ascent. Approaching the top, Ruthie said, "You know what's going to happen, don't you?"

"What do you mean?"

"To the airplane. The reason why I said you couldn't take it," she began, arriving on the balcony and remembering to stay out of sight behind the curtains.

"Oh, right." Jack looked at the plane longingly. "It's such a good one too."

"All clear," Ruthie said.

They came through the balcony door into the room— the portal back to their time—and even before they made it across to the garden door, the Vega had disappeared from Jack's hand. "Just like the arrows," Jack said.

They stood quietly for a moment on the ledge. Then Ruthie said, "Louisa could still be alive. I mean, in our time. She could be like Mrs. McVittie's age."

"If she survived the war," Jack said with a worried edge in his voice.

"What do you mean?"

"The Nazis took over Paris during World War Two. It was definitely not a safe place for anyone Jewish."

"That's terrible." Ruthie pondered what Jack had just said. If this trip back in time was like their other visits to the Thorne Rooms, she knew she had just met a person who had really lived, like Sophie Lacombe and Thomas Wilcox. She understood that she and Jack could do nothing about Amelia Earhart; her fate was sealed. But maybe they could something to help Louisa. "You know what we have to do, don't you?"

· · · 5 · · ·
LESSONS

RUTHIE WAS FILLED WITH QUESTIONS at dinner that evening. She wanted her dad to tell her all about Paris in 1937 and what had happened to the Jewish people who lived there during World War II. It was difficult to get her questions answered since her parents were busy planning her sister's upcoming trip to visit colleges.

Many of Ruthie's classmates went to cool places over spring break: exotic islands with pink sand beaches, resorts in someplace called the Mayan Riviera, or at least Florida. Ruthie, however, would be spending spring break right around the corner at Jack's while her parents and Claire traveled to college campuses. If she hadn't had other things on her mind—a real travel adventure—she would have felt completely cheated.

It was Ruthie's night to do the dishes with her dad. As he washed and she dried she could finally have his attention. He taught high school history and loved answering her questions.

"Of course you've learned about the Holocaust and the Jews who lived in Germany. But a large number left Germany in the 1930s, especially after 1935, when a set of laws limited their freedoms and citizenship. The Nazis believed that Germans were a superior race and that Jews were inferior."

"That's so crazy." Ruthie had learned all of that in school, but she still couldn't believe it. "What happened in Paris?"

"France was invaded by the Germans, and in 1940 the French surrendered. Paris was occupied by the Nazis for the duration of the war, until the American army came and liberated the city four years later."

"What happened to the Jews there?" Ruthie pressed.

"They were no safer in Paris than in Germany. Some found ways to hide, but many, many were taken off to concentration camps. And most of those people were killed."

Ruthie was beginning to feel sick. It was as though the war were happening now and she had to do something to stop it.

"You okay, sweetie?" her dad asked.

Ruthie took a deep breath. "I guess. It's just so . . . horrible."

"Yes. That's why it's important to know history—so we don't repeat it. After all, World War Two wasn't really that long ago."

Ruthie had heard her dad say stuff like that before, but

it had always gone in one ear and out the other. Now she listened and believed him. She wiped the drips off one of the china plates that her mother had inherited from her grandmother. What would it feel like if she had to leave this apartment, leave Chicago and Oakton, and be sent to a concentration camp?

Ruthie thought about Louisa and her little dog as she watched the soapsuds disappear down the drain. A realization grew in her, like a wave rising. Visiting the rooms and the past was not simply an exciting adventure; it involved matters of life and death, and she had a responsibility to do whatever she could to help Louisa.

Ruthie went to her bedroom and closed the door. She called Jack from her cell phone.

"We've got to warn her soon," Ruthie blurted out when he picked up, without even saying hello.

"Yeah. I know. Let's go back on Saturday." Jack sneezed three times on the other end of the line.

"I have my first drawing lesson on Saturday, and I don't know how long that will take. But my parents and Claire are leaving on Friday, remember? And there's no school that day anyway—it's Good Friday."

"Okay. Friday." Jack sneezed again. "I'm going to sleep now."

"Bye." Ruthie pushed the end call button but couldn't end the conversation she was having in her own head. What could they say to Louisa? How could they warn her and make her understand the danger she was in?

"Bonjour. Comment allez-vous? . . . Je m'appelle Ruthie. Comment vous appelez-vous?" Ruthie repeated after hearing the woman's voice through the earphones. She sat on her bed practicing French from a CD her mother had given her and looking at a picture book of Paris. For three nights she had practiced the language and absorbed the images, thinking it might be useful.

"Où est le parc? . . . Il fait beau aujourd'hui."

"Are you going to be doing that much longer?" Claire asked.

"Okay, okay. I'll just listen," Ruthie said as her sister climbed into bed and turned the lights out. Ruthie silently mouthed the words she heard through the earphones. They sounded beautiful. That surprised her; she was so used to French simply being what her mother taught, but she had never really listened to it. Ruthie fell asleep with the waterfall of words tumbling down into her ears.

She awoke to the sounds of general chaos in the Stewart household on Friday morning along with her cell phone ringing on her bedside table.

"Hey, Ruthie," Jack's voiced croaked at her.

"You sound awful!" Ruthie responded.

"Yeah, and I feel worse. I can't go to the museum today." He paused for a sneeze. "I have a fever, and my mom says no way. I think she wants to talk to your mom."

"Bummer." Ruthie's spirits dropped. What about Louisa? Warning her couldn't wait.

Her mom hustled into the room. "Come on, Ruthie. Time to get moving."

"Mom, Jack's sick. He has a fever and everything."

"Oh, dear!" her mother said. She conferred with Lydia on the phone. Then she made a quick call to Mrs. McVittie, who was always offering to put either of the girls up in a pinch. So it was decided that Ruthie would spend the week with Mrs. McVittie instead of with a contagious Jack.

Ruthie threw her clothes on and brushed her teeth. She had already packed her duffel with everything she needed for the week. She loved Mrs. McVittie, but as long as Jack was sick, spring break was going to be slow.

An hour later Mrs. McVittie opened the door to her apartment. "Hello, dear." A warm cinnamon aroma wafted into the hall. "Come in."

Ruthie's mom handed Mrs. McVittie their itinerary and a list of contact numbers. "Don't worry about a thing, Helen," Mrs. McVittie said. "Have a good trip."

Her mom pulled Ruthie into a huge hug. "Be good. I love you, and we'll call every night."

"Now off you go," Mrs. McVittie said, shooing her out the door.

Once Ruthie was in Mrs. McVittie's apartment she felt better. The panicky sense that she would be going stir-crazy all day began to recede. The apartment was fairly large—especially for one person—and filled with interesting objects. Mrs. McVittie had grown up in Boston but moved to Chicago as an adult. She'd lived in this apartment for over fifty years.

"Let's get you settled." Ruthie followed her down the hallway filled with old drawings in ornate frames. The guest bedroom was second on the right and had its own bathroom connected to it. *Heaven,* Ruthie thought.

"You can hang your clothes in the closet and use this chest of drawers," Mrs. McVittie said. "Then come sit with me in the kitchen."

Ruthie hadn't planned on actually hanging up her clothes, but she didn't want to insult Mrs. McVittie by leaving them in a heap in the duffel bag. She put them away in the drawers and closet. She had even packed the beaded handbag; she'd gotten into the habit of checking on it before bed, just to see if it was exhibiting a special glow. She placed it gently in the top drawer. Then Ruthie let herself fall onto the bed; of course Mrs. McVittie would have nothing but a real down comforter and pillows. She lay there and threw her arms out at her sides, feeling the feathery softness conform to her shape. She could get used to this!

Ruthie got up and walked through the apartment on her way to the kitchen. There were so many oriental rugs on the floor that they overlapped in places. A large carved stone fireplace on one wall of the living room faced another wall of tall windows with a grand piano sitting next to them—you could look out the window as you played. There were two sofas and multiple stuffed chairs, all with reading lamps next to them. The living room flowed into the dining room, where a long table was covered with piles of books.

"Sit down, Ruthie," Mrs. McVittie said when Ruthie came into the kitchen, a cozy space filled with old copper pots and well-used cookbooks. "Would you like some milk?" A plate in the middle of the table was piled high with sticky cinnamon buns.

"Yes, thank you," Ruthie said.

"It's too bad Jack is sick." Mrs. McVittie put a cold glass of milk in front of Ruthie and sat down. "Tell me—what is your newest adventure?"

Ruthie wasn't sure how Mrs. McVittie knew, but it felt natural to talk to her about everything that had happened since last Sunday. After all, Mrs. McVittie and her sister had experienced the magic in the rooms themselves when they were young. And she had helped Ruthie and Jack figure everything out by reading Sophie's French journal for them and, most important, by going along with the story about finding Mr. Bell's lost album in her storeroom. Even though Jack had already told Mrs. McVittie about the note in the bento box, Ruthie explained about her dream and how it had set everything in motion.

"You two did quite a daring thing by leaving the note in the bento box. If my sister and I had done something like that, who knows what might have happened!"

"Maybe Caroline Bell might have found it when she

was a little girl," Ruthie said. "Or maybe Jack and I might have."

"Anything is possible, isn't it?"

Then Ruthie told her about meeting Louisa Meyer outside room E27.

"You must warn her to leave Europe," Mrs. McVittie agreed. "It was a terrible time."

"I'm so worried that we won't be able to find her when we go back. Or what if we can't convince her? We're just kids."

"You will find a way, I don't doubt. Wait—I have an idea." Mrs. McVittie rose from her chair. "Follow me."

Ruthie followed her back through the apartment and down the hall past the guest room and a study, into her bedroom. Mrs. McVittie opened a door to the most enormous closet Ruthie had ever seen. Inside were hundreds of articles of clothing, neatly arranged on racks that filled the entire space.

"It used to be a third bedroom, but I had it converted to a closet. You can see why," she explained.

"Mrs. McVittie, where did you get all these clothes?"

"Some are mine, and some I've collected because they were beautiful." She walked along one wall and pulled out a dress. "I wore this when I was about your age." She held up a blue dress with a white collar and sash and puffy sleeves. "I think this would fit you. Here, try it on."

Ruthie took it off the hanger and slipped it on over her T-shirt and jeans. It fit, but when she glanced in the mirror she wasn't so sure about the style—she thought it made her look like a six-year-old!

"Isn't this fun?" Mrs. McVittie said. "I remember wearing that dress. Here, how about this one?" She handed Ruthie a yellow one, without puffy sleeves and with a differently shaped collar and patch pockets. A black Scottie dog silhouette was stitched near the bottom. Ruthie admired herself in the mirror. This dress looked kind of cool in a vintage way.

"I think that is just the one," Mrs. McVittie said. "You should wear it when you go to find Louisa. You'll fit right in."

"That's a great idea, Mrs. McVittie. Thanks!"

"I might have something to fit Jack too, with a little luck." She rummaged through the closet and pulled out a pair of light-colored pants that had a different cut than Jack's usual cargo pants, a white polo shirt, and a green V-neck sweater. She even had shoes to match. "These belonged to a cousin of mine. I think they're charming!"

"I don't know if Jack will wear these," Ruthie said doubtfully. "But they look like they'll fit."

Mrs. McVittie was tireless, and they spent a long while looking through all the clothes, which were organized by decade. Drawers filled to overflowing contained all kinds of accessories; jewelry, scarves and handbags spanning more than seventy years. It made the time pass on what could have been a very slow day.

.   .   .

Ruthie took a cab to the museum Saturday morning and loved the freedom of riding in one by herself. Soon she was climbing the grand steps with her cell phone to her ear, Mrs. McVittie's voice reminding her to call again when her lesson was over. She went directly to the meeting place by the information desk just inside the front doors.

Dora Pommeroy was already waiting. Ruthie observed her stylish clothing—skinny dark jeans, a silky turquoise T-shirt and a light-colored jacket with lots of gold buttons. Several strands of pearls and beads were looped loosely around her neck, along with an Art Institute ID tag. Her shiny, white-blond hair was pulled back, like before, and she wore a different pair of cool glasses. Ruthie was wearing regular jeans, another Oakton T-shirt, and her sweatshirt. She felt so boring.

"Good morning, Ruthie!" Dora smiled and looked at her watch. "You're right on time. Excellent! Shall we get started?" Ruthie made a mental note to always be on time for Dora since it seemed to please her.

Dora flashed her ID at the guards as she walked past the entrance, Ruthie following.

"Before we begin," Dora said, stopping at a bench near the grand staircase, "let's go over the supplies I've brought for you."

Ruthie watched as Dora pulled art supplies from an enormous leather tote bag: a sketchbook (on which she had already written Ruthie's name), a small metal pencil case containing six artist's pencils, a squishy gray gum eraser, and something that looked like a pencil but was really a stick of rolled-up paper, called a smudger, for shading. Dora explained how to use each item.

Probably because it was the first Saturday of spring break, the museum wasn't very crowded. They went downstairs into Gallery 11, which was emptier than Ruthie had ever seen it during the day.

"This is great," Dora said. "We'll be able to linger over one room for a long time without annoying anyone. Do you have a favorite?"

"Every time I pick a favorite, it changes as soon as I look at another room!" Ruthie answered.

"I know; me too!" Dora agreed. "Let's start with the basics: one object." She moved down the wall, needing to bend to look through the glass, and stopped at room E1. "Why don't you pick something from this room?"

Christina's room!

"Would you like to start with a different one?"

"No. This one is fine," Ruthie tried to say casually. It was, after all, the first room, but the choice made her uneasy.

"How about that stand there, with the beautiful book on it near the window?"

Christina's book! Ruthie caught herself before she made an audible gulp. She and Jack had learned all about the magic of the key from this book—a book filled with so much magic that it had carried the voice of the young duchess across the centuries for Ruthie to hear. It would be hard for her to stand there and keep calm while trying to pretend it was just a run-of-the-mill miniature.

"On second thought," Dora began, moving down the wall a few windows, "let's start with something simpler. Here, room E5."

Ruthie went along, relieved. The room was a cottage kitchen from England in the early 1700s. "I think I could draw this." She pointed to an unadorned table on the right-hand side of the room. A small blue pitcher and a common white bowl sat on it. Next to the table a bay window looked out onto a beautiful garden bursting with flowers, and she could see neighboring houses. Across the room, an open door piqued Ruthie's imagination. Where did it lead? Was this world alive? It appeared perfectly still, but if she had the key and were inside . . .

Ruthie got to work while Dora opened her own sketchbook to draw along with her. Dora instructed her to do the best job she could so she could see her skill level. When she was finished, Ruthie handed her sketch to Dora.

"Very good! I think you have a feel for this!"

Ruthie beamed. They spent about a half hour on this room, drawing a plain wooden chair and a candlestick, Dora giving drawing tips as Ruthie sketched. She looked at Dora's pages. "Yours are *sooo* good."

"Practice. But you know, when you love something, it comes easily. And I love these rooms!"

"So do I!" Ruthie felt a bond with Dora, which kind of

surprised her. How could Ruthie have anything in common with an elegant person like Dora Pommeroy?

Dora let Ruthie pick a few more rooms to work on, and the two of them talked as they sketched. She was so easy to talk to, and Ruthie found herself getting very comfortable with her—more comfortable than she'd been with any teacher before. Since Dora was doing her own research about the rooms, she was excited to hear about the paper Ruthie and Jack had written for Ms. Biddle. Ruthie told her everything she remembered learning from the archives.

"I should make you my research assistant." Dora laughed. "You remind me of myself at your age!"

"Have you ever decorated a room to look exactly like any of the Thorne Rooms?" Ruthie asked, sketching a vase from room E26.

"I'd love to try, but it is difficult these days to find antiques as wonderful as the objects Mrs. Thorne created. If you can find them, they're very expensive," Dora explained.

"This is one of my favorites," Ruthie said as they approached E27.

"I love this one too," Dora agreed. "I love the view of Paris over the balcony."

"My dad was telling me about this period in history. It was pretty scary."

"But the design style was fabulous: high modernist." Dora changed the subject. "Now, I'll have time to see you tomorrow for another lesson if you'd like. I'll show you how to use one-point perspective, and you can practice till the next lesson. Okay?"

"Okay." Ruthie was disappointed that the lesson was over.

Dora walked her upstairs and out of the museum to help her hail a cab for the short ride back to Mrs. McVittie's. Waiting for the traffic light in front of the museum to turn green, Ruthie watched through the window as Dora strode effortlessly up the stone steps and disappeared back inside.

... 6 ...
CONFESSIONS

JACK'S VOICE SOUNDED LIKE SANDPAPER on wood. Ruthie had called him right after she had talked to her parents on the phone and helped Mrs. McVittie clean up the dinner dishes.

"Actually, I'm feeling a little better. I slept till dinner," he told her. "And my temperature's almost normal. Probably one more day."

"That's great. I was worried you'd be sick for all of spring break," Ruthie said. "I'll come over after my lesson tomorrow."

"Oh, I almost forgot—she's coming over tomorrow," Jack said as an afterthought.

"Who? Dora?"

"Yeah," Jack answered.

"Why?" Ruthie felt a prickle of jealousy.

"She wants to talk to my mom about painting some

mural. For some rich lady's apartment that she's decorating or something."

The explanation made Ruthie feel better and, in fact, amplified her excitement; she might get to learn more about how Dora worked if Lydia was going to be involved. But still, it was just like Jack to have such good luck and hardly notice it at all.

Ruthie went to sleep that night with French words streaming through the headphones. The lesson was all about food and dining, and she heard phrases such as *"Je voudrais manger une pomme, s'il vous plaît"* and *"La viande est délicieuse."* She wasn't sure if "I would like to eat an apple, please" or "The meat is delicious" would come in handy in 1937 Paris, but she had to start somewhere. As she drifted off, the sounds of the words turned into pictures in her head and she saw the letters *v-i-a-n-d-e* floating by, and then *p-o-m-m-e* morphed into shiny apples bobbing like a dancing chorus line over the bed. Soon she was dreaming of rooms and tables and pencils. More juicy-looking apples appeared; Ruthie tried to grab one, but they were just out of reach.

Ruthie remembered to arrive on time—actually a few minutes early—for her drawing lesson on Sunday. Dora's height and long stride made her stand out among the crowd of people, and Ruthie waved to her. Dora checked her watch as she had yesterday and smiled in approval.

"You're early!" she said in greeting.

"I hate being late," Ruthie responded.

"Me too! We seem to have a lot in common." Dora looked over Ruthie's practice sketches and gave her comments and a few pointers. Again, they chatted while they worked; she appeared genuinely interested in everything Ruthie had to say. After they had sketched for some time—Ruthie worked on a New England bedroom with a canopy bed—Dora made an offer.

"How would you like to see the installation? I mean in the corridor behind the rooms. I need to make a few notes for my own research about how the rooms were constructed, and I don't think it would be a problem for me to show you."

Ruthie tried to look excited, though she had already been in the corridor many times. "Sure, that would be great."

"I have use of the key. The archivist gave me authorization." Dora dangled the key like a fishing lure.

Stepping into the corridor, Ruthie heard the familiar sound of the door locking automatically as it shut.

It was odd to be in the corridor with someone other than Jack. Ruthie pretended she had never seen any of this before. They walked along to the first turn, just steps away from the duct-tape climbing strip. Ruthie had devised this a few months ago so she and Jack—after shrinking—could climb up and crawl through the heating duct to reach the corridor that ran behind the American rooms. She hoped Dora wouldn't notice it.

"Just like you, I've learned loads of fascinating things in the archive. Mrs. Thorne was meticulous about explaining the details," Dora said. "But what surprises me most are some of the unexplained aspects."

"I know," Ruthie agreed.

"Did you come across her notes about the secret shop in Paris?"

"Yeah. Jack and I were really interested in that!"

"Yes! So intriguing!" Dora responded. "And did you find any documents about a key?"

Ruthie's stomach tensed, but she was able to answer truthfully. "No. We didn't find any documents about a key."

"That's too bad. I found a couple of obscure references to a very old key that one of her craftsmen acquired. They seemed to think it was extremely important. I was hoping maybe . . . ," she began, but just then they arrived at the climbing strip. Ruthie's stomach clenched even more.

"Look at this." Dora stopped to examine the vertical oddity. "What on earth could it be?"

Ruthie kept quiet.

"Hmmm," Dora murmured, observing how three lengths of tape ran from the ground to the air vent. She touched the three strips. "This center one has the sticky side out." She turned and aimed her very blue eyes at Ruthie. "Any theories?"

Ruthie shrugged.

"I should probably say something to the staff about this." Dora kept staring at Ruthie.

"Maybe you shouldn't," Ruthie finally blurted out.

"Why not? Whatever it is doesn't belong here," Dora said logically.

"I don't know." Ruthie wished she'd stayed quiet.

"Ruthie?" Dora asked in a voice that Ruthie's mother might use when Ruthie was being less than truthful. "Is something wrong?"

Ruthie stood there in the dim light of the corridor not sure what to say. She was a terrible liar! *If only Jack were here,* she thought, *he'd have some convincing story ready.*

"No, nothing's wrong."

Dora continued to look at the climbing strip. "Yes, it should be removed. It's collecting dust." She used a fingernail to pull it off the wall some, but the duct tape held fast. "Anyway," she said, working away at the adhesive, "the references to the key in the archive really got me to thinking. You know, I just have the feeling it's a key to something important and no one seems to know anything about it. Maybe it's been lost."

Ruthie could feel the blood rushing to her face; she might as well have had the word *guilty* written across her forehead. Dora noticed. "Ruthie, are you sure you didn't come across something when you were doing your research?"

Ruthie stayed mute and frozen while Dora looked at her.

"Ruthie?"

The hum from the diorama lights seemed to blare in

the silence. "I don't think you'll believe me if I tell you," Ruthie said.

"Try me," Dora said.

And so Ruthie began. "I do know something about that key. . . ."

She only meant to tell her a little. But Dora looked so interested and listened so patiently that the whole story of the key, the magic and the shrinking just spilled right out.

When she was finished, Dora was thoughtful for a moment. "It's quite a story! It's hard to believe. . . . I shouldn't believe it. . . . But I want to because of what I've learned in my own research. Mrs. Thorne left some big hints about magic."

Ruthie was more than relieved. It would have felt horrible if Dora had thought Ruthie was just some nutty kid who made things up.

"Your secret is safe with me," Dora vowed.

"We're going to return the key. We just don't know where to put it yet," Ruthie clarified.

"I hope you're keeping the key in a safe place."

"We are. Jack has it." Ruthie remembered how she'd felt when they had confided in Mrs. McVittie, reassured and grateful that she had someone else to talk to about it all.

Dora smiled at her. "I'm glad you decided to tell me."

Ruthie noted a different feeling when they returned to the gallery. She had revealed something important to Dora—something huge—and now she wondered if they would still be teacher and student. Ruthie very awkwardly asked if they could continue this lesson.

Dora checked her watch. "Yes, we can work for about another half hour, and then I have an appointment."

"With Lydia?" Ruthie asked.

"That's right. Did Jack tell you?"

"Yes. And I'm supposed to go to his house this afternoon too."

"Then why don't we go together?" Dora suggested. "How perfect!"

"Okay." Ruthie looked down at her drawing, which was less than perfect so far. Maybe if she hung around Dora enough, some perfection would rub off on her.

"It's so nice to see you again." Lydia welcomed Dora—and Ruthie—into the loft.

"Your work came to mind immediately when my client suggested a trompe l'oeil painting," Dora enthused. Then she saw Jack in the doorway of his room. "Hello again. What a wonderful loft. And, Jack, you have your own house!"

Ruthie always loved to witness people seeing Jack and Lydia's loft for the first time. It had originally been a factory space, and Lydia redesigned everything for them to live there. They had a great view of the city through really tall windows. The loft was a big L-shaped space; one leg was Lydia's studio, and the other leg was their living area, in which Jack had his own two-story "house," with a door and windows looking out to the rest of the loft. He'd painted and decorated it as he pleased. It was fantastic.

"Show her what it's like inside," she prompted Jack. Dora followed Jack as he led a tour of his house, with its downstairs living room and upstairs sleeping loft. When they came back out, Lydia offered Dora some iced tea, and the two of them walked around the corner into Lydia's studio.

Jack plopped down at the kitchen table. "I can't go back in my room. I've been in there too long." A layer cake sat on a cake stand on the table. "Want some?"

"Sure. I wish my mom baked as much as yours!" Ruthie said.

Jack sliced two large wedges and placed them on plates.

"I've had such a great time with Dora the past two days. You'll really like her," Ruthie said.

"Really? Why?"

Ruthie thought it should be obvious to Jack, but then of course he hardly knew Dora at all. As she let the chocolate frosting melt in her mouth she also realized she would have to tell him that she had revealed almost everything to Dora. Her throat tightened a bit.

"Well, she's really trustworthy."

"I thought she was just teaching you to draw," he said, taking another bite.

"Yeah, but we talk. And we have so much in common."

Jack looked skeptical. "What could you have in

common with her? I mean, she's nice and all, but look at her!"

Ruthie was a little insulted, but she had to admit that on the surface, she and Dora did seem very different. "Well, we both love the Thorne Rooms."

"Lots of people love them. And how do you know she's trustworthy?"

"I don't know. It's just . . . I can tell her stuff."

Jack shrugged. "Hey, come look at this." He hopped out of his chair, and Ruthie followed him into the living room of his house. He opened the lid on his always running laptop and punched a few keys on it; a live overhead shot of the two of them looking at his computer appeared on the monitor.

"How'd you do that?"

Jack pointed to a camera smaller than a spool of thread that sat on top of the door frame. It didn't look like a camera; in fact, it was only the lens and a small transmitter, he explained. "I rigged up my own personal security system. I was so bored this morning, and then I started thinking about that art thief. I already had all the junk I needed to do it."

"Cool!" Ruthie mugged for the camera.

"It's wireless. I could put it anywhere in the apartment—within a certain range, though." He pushed a few more keys. "Now it's recording to a disk."

"I'm impressed. Was it hard to do?"

"Naw. My uncle sent me the camera and software for

my last birthday, and I hadn't gotten around to trying it. I just went online for some technical advice."

Jack was the only person she knew who could possibly figure out how to do this all by himself while home sick.

"Let's finish the cake. Being sick makes you hungry." He closed the lid on his laptop.

Back in the kitchen, Jack shoved another large bite of cake in his mouth. "Milk?" he asked, getting up again.

Ruthie nodded.

"Shoot!" he said, scanning the fridge. "We're all out. I'm gonna tell my mom—she should let me out of the house to go get milk, since it's just three blocks away."

Lydia granted permission, and as they walked to the grocery store, Ruthie felt the weight of guilt bearing down on her. She had to tell Jack what she had done this morning, but she wasn't sure how to say it. She stared at the sidewalk.

"I hate being sick; it's great to be out of the house!" Jack rejoiced. When Ruthie didn't respond, he commented, "You're kinda quiet all of a sudden."

"I know," she said tentatively. "Guess where Dora took me today?"

"I give up. Where?"

"The corridor."

"Anything happen?"

"Sort of." A skateboarder careened by, nearly running into Jack, and they both had to dodge.

"Hey, watch out!" Jack called. Then he turned his attention back to Ruthie. "What do you mean, sort of?"

"She saw the climbing strip."

"So?"

"I told her."

Jack stopped in his tracks. "You told her *what*?"

"About the magic."

"Are you serious?"

"Don't be mad. She kinda already knew about the key. She read something about it in the archives. And she's going to keep it a secret."

"So that's why you said she's trustworthy?"

"She is."

"I hope so. I can't believe you did that. And without even talking to me first!"

"I wish I hadn't, but it just happened. She could tell I was hiding something, and you know I can't lie!"

"Keeping quiet isn't the same thing as lying!" He walked off in front of her a few paces. He was steaming. She could barely keep up with him as he stomped into the store and down the cereal aisle to the dairy case in the back. He grabbed a gallon of milk.

"Jack!" she started. He scowled at her and went back to the cereal aisle.

After a few seconds that seemed like minutes, he took a deep breath, exhaling loudly but not saying anything. Ruthie continued, "Look, I'm sorry. But maybe it's not a bad thing."

"Well, whether it is or isn't, it's done." He walked slowly, looking over the cereal choices.

"I really am sorry I told her without you. And I promise never to do something like that again."

"Okay, okay." He reached for a box of cereal. "Here, you hold the milk." He handed it off to her. The lines were long at the checkout, and it gave Jack more time to mellow before they had to return to his house.

Back out on the sidewalk, Ruthie decided to refocus his attention by telling him about Mrs. McVittie's clothing collection. "So we could both have the right clothes to wear when we go back to find Louisa," she finished after telling him about the two perfect period outfits.

"When do you want to go?" he asked, almost completely over his angry storm. "I don't think my mom will let me go tomorrow. Better try Tuesday."

"Yeah, that'll be good for me. I wish we could go right now to warn her. I'm so worried that we're not going to be able to find her."

They had reached Jack's building. He was resisting going inside again, so they sat on the front steps for a few minutes. "You know this means we have to put her on the list," Jack said.

"What do you mean?"

"We know Dora has access to the rooms."

"Yeah, but—"

Jack interrupted her. "I've been thinking. Now that

Mrs. McVittie and Dora know, maybe you're right about talking to Dr. Bell."

Ruthie was glad he had been the one to bring this up. "I think it's a good idea. I got the feeling when we met her at the opening that she wants to know more," she said. "We can see if she'll meet with us before we go to the museum on Tuesday."

Jack looked up at the blue sky. "I don't want to go back inside. It's so nice out. I guess it's not that bad not going on some swanky island vacation for spring break. At least we get to go to Paris!"

"And do something important, like save someone's life," Ruthie added with a big grin.

· · · 7 · · ·

THE SILVER BOX

"'**D**R. CAROLINE BELL, M.D,'" **JACK** read on the office
door. "This is the place."

The receptionist ushered them into an office filled
with medical books, Dr. Bell's diplomas and some photos
of her with her father. Ruthie also noticed a beautiful one
of Dr. Bell as a baby in her mother's arms. She recognized
it as one of the photos they had rediscovered.

"Hello, Ruthie. Hello, Jack," Dr. Bell said, entering the
office and shaking hands. She sat down at her desk. "It's so
nice to see you both again. Please have a seat." Ruthie felt
the warmth from her smile. "So what did you want to see
me about?"

Ruthie began, "At the opening of your dad's exhibition
you said you thought we had more to talk about."

"What do you think?" Dr. Bell asked.

"I think you want to know more about how we found

your backpack," Ruthie suggested, hoping Dr. Bell would get the hint. She must have memories, Ruthie thought, just like Mrs. McVittie's, about going into the rooms as a child, memories that she had a hard time believing. Finding Dr. Bell's belongings—the backpack filled with her schoolbooks and her father's photo album—hidden all those years in the tiny cabinet of room E17 had given Ruthie and Jack the proof that she had experienced the magic.

Dr. Bell studied their faces for a moment. "Let me show you something," she said. She swiveled her desk chair and took something from the bookshelves behind her. It was a small silver box, about three inches square, with intricate decorations carved into the lid. She handed it to Ruthie, who turned it over in her hand like an antiques expert. Looking at the markings on the bottom, she saw some letters and a lion.

"It's from England," Ruthie said confidently. When Dr. Bell looked surprised, Ruthie added, "Mrs. McVittie taught me how to read the markings. Where did you get it?"

"I'm not sure; I've had it for as long as I can remember, though." She looked at it thoughtfully. "I once had a dream about it being from a dollhouse and growing in the palm of my hand."

"That was no dream, Dr. Bell," Jack put in.

"What do you mean?"

"I mean that it probably did grow in your hand. And that the stories you told your dad when you were a little girl—about shrinking and going into the Thorne Rooms—all that really happened."

"This little box is probably from one of the rooms," Ruthie concluded.

Again the room was quiet. Dr. Bell's gaze was directed at the box in her hand, although her focus was far away.

"I was just a little girl with an active imagination." After a few moments she looked at them, tears welling in her eyes. "I'm a doctor—a scientist. I shouldn't believe this."

"We couldn't believe it either," Ruthie said gently, "but it happened to us. We shrank and went into the rooms."

"That's where we—Ruthie, actually—found your backpack," Jack said.

"In a cabinet in one of the bedrooms with a canopy bed," Ruthie added.

Dr. Bell gave a small chuckle. "I was obsessed with that bed." She thought some more. "But I still can't believe all this is true. How can it be?"

"There was a magic key that a duchess named Christina of Milan had made centuries ago," Jack explained.

Dr. Bell's expression registered a memory. "Yes! I remember a beautiful shining key!"

"Christina had the key created so she could make herself almost invisible. We read about it in a book she wrote that's in one of the rooms," Jack continued.

"But it's all so impossible!"

"Why do you think you kept this little box all these

years? Deep down you must have known your memories were real," Ruthie said.

Dr. Bell smiled. "You're very insightful, aren't you?"

Ruthie shrugged. "It happened to our friend Mrs. McVittie too, a long time ago."

"The rooms—and, I suppose, the magic—helped me get through those difficult times when my mother died." Dr. Bell sighed heavily. "Now I've got to pull myself together and get back to work. I wish I had more time to talk. I have a lot to think about." She stood up and walked around to the door. "I want to thank you both so much for everything you've done, for me and my father. He's never been happier since he's gotten back to his photography."

"We were just lucky," Ruthie said.

"Before you go . . ." Dr. Bell went back to her desk and picked up the beautiful box, cradling it in her hand for a moment. "I think I remember which room this came from now. It was a grand dining room. I think the walls were pale green, with lots of white decorations." She paused, her memories seeming to become clearer. "And I remember a funny white statue of a lady with a bow and arrow."

"I know which room that is," Ruthie said.

"Perhaps you'll do me the favor of returning it? To put it back where it belongs?"

"No problem," Jack answered.

Ruthie and Jack left her office. Out in the hallway Jack

said, "We can rule her out. She didn't write the note, for sure."

"And I don't think she can help us figure out who did," Ruthie replied.

"I can't believe I forgot the key!" Jack griped as they were getting off the bus near his building.

"We had to come back this way anyway," Ruthie said. One block later they were at his door. "I'm glad we talked to her."

"Yeah. She seemed relieved to know what really happened to her when she was a kid. Just like Mrs. McVittie."

The elevator brought them up to Jack's floor. Lydia had left a note for Jack on the kitchen table, saying she had an appointment and would be back by dinner. "I'll just get the key and then we can go to the museum," he said.

Ruthie had the clothes they were going to change into stuffed into her canvas bag, along with the climbing ladder. She double-checked to make sure she had everything while she waited for Jack, who seemed to be taking an extra couple of minutes to retrieve the key. He appeared from his room, his face ashen.

"What's wrong?" Ruthie asked.

"I can't find it! It's not where I put it!"

"What do you mean?" She charged into his room. "Let me look."

They went through the shoe box again, pulling every

item out; it wasn't there. They looked through every drawer, under his bed, even in it. The key was nowhere!

"Think—when did you last see it?"

"When we used it last Tuesday. I put it back; I'm sure I did!"

"Does your mom have a new cleaning person or anything like that?"

"No," Jack answered, thoroughly perplexed. They were quiet for a long moment, minds racing. "There's one other possibility. My mom took some stuff to the dry cleaner the other day, including the jacket I was wearing on Tuesday. I'm sure I put the key in the box, but maybe . . . maybe I didn't."

"Which dry cleaner?"

"She always uses the one around the corner."

"Let's go!" Ruthie sprinted for the elevator, and Jack was right behind her. They sped out to the street and around the block, swinging open the door of the cleaner's. Jack rang the service bell on the counter several times. While they waited, Ruthie noticed a sign next to the cash register. In red lettering it stated, Not Responsible for Valuables Left in Pockets.

"Coming, coming!" A man's voice sounded from behind the curtain of plastic garment bags hanging on the conveyor.

Jack called out, "My mom brought some clothes here the other day. I think I might have left something in the pocket."

Finally the clothing parted and the man appeared. He had a large wrench in his hand and didn't look too happy. "Darn thing broke down again!"

"Please," Jack began. "I need to look in the pocket of my jacket."

"You got your ticket?"

"No. But this is an emergency."

"He lost something important," Ruthie chimed in.

"I can't help you without the ticket."

"Please!" they said simultaneously.

The man sighed. "What'd ya lose?"

"A key," Jack said.

"House? Car?" the man asked.

"Uh, neither. It's an antique key."

The man didn't respond but disappeared into the back. He returned carrying a box, about triple the size of a shoe box. He set it heavily on the counter.

"We got keys. You're welcome to look through them. We always check pockets. Keys go in this box. I can't promise it's in there." He disappeared again through the plastic-covered clothes. They heard the clanking of metal.

"There are hundreds in here!" Ruthie felt discouraged.

"Start digging. If our key is in here, it will stand out." Jack plunged his hand into the pile.

Ruthie had never known there were so many different sizes and shapes of keys. They all blurred together after a while. Soon it became evident to both of them that their key was not in this box.

"Sir," Jack called, "could I please take a look at my jacket pocket? The key isn't here."

The man came back to the counter and leaned forward. "I got big problems today. If you think I can find your jacket without your ticket, I got news for you. We got hundreds of items here."

"Could we look?" Ruthie asked.

"No clients behind the counter." He softened somewhat when he saw the look of desperation on Ruthie's face. "Look, I'm sorry. We got strict rules. My workers always check pockets. Though I hate to say it, sometimes valuables don't end up in the box. Some people don't respect personal property as much as they should."

"Finders keepers," Jack sighed.

"That's what the sign's for." He gestured with the wrench to the red-lettered sign. "Now I gotta get this thing fixed." He left for good this time.

"This is horrible!" Ruthie choked back the lump forming in her throat.

"Really, I'm pretty sure I didn't leave it in the pocket." Jack sounded like he was trying to convince both Ruthie and himself. They returned to the sidewalk and trudged back to the loft.

In the elevator Ruthie said, "I could get used to never being able to shrink again, I guess. But I can't stand the idea of not warning Louisa to get out of Paris. Her life is at stake!"

"I know, I know! Let's keep looking."

"You don't think there was something about the magic itself that made it disappear?" Ruthie pondered aloud as they looked everywhere in the loft for the third time. "Like maybe we kept it too long or something." Ruthie had secretly worried about this. After all, the key didn't belong to them.

"I guess it's possible. I mean, who ever thought any of this could happen in the first place?" Jack continued looking in his mother's studio while Ruthie combed through trash cans and kitchen cabinets. They spent the next two hours searching everywhere, but it appeared the key had truly vanished.

Ruthie had pains in her side as she and Jack stood at the door to Mrs. McVittie's apartment, panting. They hadn't waited for the bus. Instead, they'd run along the sidewalks, turning the usual twenty-minute walk into a ten-minute sprint. Now she pushed the buzzer several times. Mrs. McVittie opened the door and stared at them, startled.

"Goodness! What's wrong?" she asked.

"It's gone . . . the key . . . we . . . can't find it." Ruthie could barely talk, she was so out of breath. "Mrs. McVittie . . . how are we going to . . . warn Louisa?"

"Sit down, both of you, catch your breath." Mrs. McVittie walked them into the living room. "Now, one at a time, tell me what this is about." She listened patiently as they recounted everything.

Finally Mrs. McVittie interrupted their blast of words

and worry. "Calm down. All this upset won't make the key reappear. Perhaps if we start to think logically and observe carefully, we'll find clues that may lead to answers."

"Observe what carefully?" Ruthie questioned, her voice tinged with fear.

"Everything. Go back to your research paper, to the Thorne Rooms, to the catalogue, to your memory. I will do the same. Some small thing unnoticed may tell you more than you can imagine. Question your assumptions." She looked at the two sitting glumly in her cushiony chairs. "All is not lost."

Ruthie climbed into bed that night emotionally exhausted. Trying to take Mrs. McVittie's advice, she went over the recent events as if her life were a movie, replaying moments, looking at things from new angles, hoping to see a glimpse of the key. But it only reminded her of the possibility of never finding it again.

She was so worried about Louisa. Could she live with the knowledge that she had had the chance to save someone and then blew it? And it wasn't just Louisa—it was her whole family. She put her headphones on. Letting the French words soak into her memory as she repeated them, she had some trouble with the phrase *"Je regrette"*—"I'm sorry."

Ruthie tossed and turned as she slept. She dreamed she was standing in front of the horrible building she had seen in Paris, the one with the frightening eagle on the top. The stone bird suddenly came to life, swooped down and chased her, only instead of being pursued through the streets of Paris, she was running through her neighborhood in Chicago. The swoosh of its massive wings over her head and the gusts they created nearly knocked her off her feet. The sharp claws had just grazed her shoulders, piercing her shirt. She sat up in bed, a cold sweat on her forehead. It was dawn.

Grateful that she had awoken to escape the talons of the predator bird, Ruthie got out of bed and used the bathroom. She wanted to go back to sleep, but she needed something to calm her. Then she thought of the beaded handbag. Ruthie took it out of the drawer and climbed back into bed with it, adjusting the pillow and angling herself so that the faint early-morning light shone through the window right onto the handbag.

The beads sparkled, and Ruthie felt slightly hypnotized by the rainbows bouncing off the facets. It looked so much more impressive than the handbags she'd seen in department stores. This one dazzled. She turned it over and over, following the floral design as it wound its way intricately around the bag. Was this what Mrs. McVittie had had in mind when she'd said to observe everything carefully?

And then she felt it. There was no doubt this time. It was warming in her hand, first just at her fingertips, then spreading to her palms. *I knew it!* she thought.

Soon it was sparkling even more intensely. She didn't look away, thinking that if she stopped staring at the bag, the warming would cease. But it didn't cool down, and for a good ten minutes the handbag seemed almost alive, as if it were trying to tell her something. Did the bag have a kind of magic triggered by something unknown to her? Or was it like a hibernating animal rousing? She had no idea why this was happening now. Finally it cooled to normal and the glinting dimmed. She rolled onto her back and lay clutching the bag, listening to the first chirping birds outside.

When Ruthie woke up again, it was nearly eight o'clock, and the bag was still in her hands. The songs of the birds had been replaced by sounds coming from the kitchen. She jumped out of bed, taking the bag with her to find Mrs. McVittie.

"Good morning, dear. Did you sleep well?" Mrs. McVittie was cracking eggs into a mixing bowl.

"I had a horrible dream about being chased by a giant eagle," Ruthie began. "It woke me up, but then I took this out of the drawer." She held up the handbag for Mrs. McVittie to see. "And it warmed in my hand! It was glowing too!"

"Are you sure?" Mrs. McVittie asked, but without any serious doubt in her voice.

"I'm positive. The night you gave it to me I thought it did the same thing, but I wasn't sure—I thought maybe I imagined it. But this morning it lasted a long time. Mrs. McVittie, where did it come from?"

"I don't know precisely. It was my sister's and she prized it. She never would let me touch it and never said where she got it. It was in a box of things I inherited when she died. Packed away for years!" Her brows were knitted for a moment. "I wonder . . ."

"What, Mrs. McVittie?"

"It's very possible that she actually stole it from one of the rooms and never told me. It would have been easy for her to slip it in her pocket, since we took turns going into the rooms. We never went in them together, because one of us had to lift the other to enter."

"But which room do you think it might have come from?"

"Why don't you get dressed and we'll do a little research after breakfast."

As Ruthie dressed she had a renewed sense of optimism. She wondered how old the bag really was and how much magic it held. By the time she'd finished her omelet, Ruthie had convinced herself that the handbag would somehow lead to answers—and to Louisa.

Mrs. McVittie had her own copy of the Thorne Rooms catalogue, and the two of them pored over the pictures of every room to see if they could find any pattern, any decorative motif that resembled the handbag. Ruthie felt discouraged when, after scanning the last of the European room pages, they had found nothing.

"I'm not at all surprised. I've always thought the style more American," Mrs. McVittie reassured her.

Sure enough, when they turned the page to a South Carolina ballroom, room A29, they were both immediately struck by the patterns on the rug and the color scheme of the room. Soft green, peach and gold echoed the colors of the beads, and the floral shapes of the rug repeated those of the bag. It was not an exact match, but the handbag wouldn't have looked out of place in the room.

"Of course, the photos in this catalogue were all taken long after my sister and I had visited the rooms," Mrs. McVittie said, gazing for a long time at the picture. "Yes, we were in this room. I'm certain of it."

"I've got to tell Jack. We need to bring the handbag into the corridor and see what happens!"

··· 8 ···

SOMETHING FOUND

FRUSTRATINGLY, JACK HAD A MAKEUP piano lesson that morning, and then Lydia made him stay home for lunch. He finally arrived at Mrs. McVittie's a little after two, and they hurried to the museum. Ruthie was dizzy with the possibilities of what might happen, but Jack reminded her that without Christina's key they would have to find just the right moment to sneak into the corridor the old-fashioned way—with the non-magic Art Institute key. The risk of getting caught was great. Ruthie tried not to let this dampen her mood.

Neither of them had a backpack to check, so they made their way swiftly to the lower level, the small beaded handbag safely in Ruthie's messenger bag. They entered Gallery 11 and went straight to room A29.

Less than ten seconds later Ruthie whispered, "It's

getting warm. I can feel it through the canvas, Jack!" She discreetly opened the bag and they both looked inside.

Even with no light hitting it, the smaller handbag glowed, the beads sparkling like diamonds. They could feel the heat emanating from it. The light bounced off the other items in her bag, all dull in comparison.

Ruthie closed the messenger bag and looked around to see if anyone was watching.

"Come over here." She led Jack out of Gallery 11 to a small side room where computers and chairs were set up for kids. It was empty, and Ruthie thought they wouldn't be noticed. "What should we do? I'm afraid to touch it. It's still warm, even out here."

"I think I should touch it first."

"Okay, but really quickly." She opened her messenger bag.

Jack looked around, then placed his hand inside and touched the glowing beads with one finger. Nothing happened, so he reached his hand around the object, as if to grab it.

"Funny, I can feel the warmth around it, but when I touch it, it feels pretty much room temperature." He left his hand on it for a minute, waiting. "You try it."

Ruthie slowly lowered her index finger. She quickly pulled it out. "Hot, really hot, Jack!"

"Awesome! Do it again."

She repeated the motion, leaving her finger on longer.

"It's not spreading; it's only hot where I have contact." She kept her finger on it. "Just like Christina's book."

"Do you hear anything?"

She listened for a moment to see if she would hear the magical bell sounds that they'd heard standing in front of Christina's book. "No. Nothing."

They sat for a minute or two, attempting to figure out what the glowing object was trying to tell them. "Let me see it close up," Jack said.

"You take it out," Ruthie suggested.

Jack reached into her messenger bag and lifted the jeweled handbag. He turned his back to the main room so that anyone walking by wouldn't be able to see the light coming from his lap. The handbag had a small clasp with a ruby-red rhinestone holding it closed. He pressed on it and the bag opened. The interior was lined with gold satin, which nearly blinded them with a burst of light.

"Oh!" was all Ruthie could say as the glow lit up Jack's face. The luminosity appeared to be radiating from one spot underneath the gold fabric.

"I think there's something in there," Jack said, fingering the fabric. "I feel something hard."

"Are you sure? Maybe you're just feeling the beadwork from the other side."

"No. It feels different, like something flat, maybe a large coin." He reached into his pocket and pulled out his Swiss army knife. He pulled the scissor implement from its slot.

"What are you doing, Jack? You can't cut it!" Ruthie was horrified.

"I'll just undo the stitching along the inside seam. We can stitch it back up."

"You'll ruin it!" Ruthie cried.

"Someone hid something in the lining and we need to find out what it is! I'll be super careful," he promised.

Ruthie's mind spun. Someone had hidden something? What? Who? "Okay." She breathed deeply.

Jack deftly cut the tiny threads of the inside seam, avoiding any damage to the fabric. When he'd cut about an inch he wiggled his finger in. He looked at Ruthie with a grin.

"What is it?"

"I don't know yet." He made a few more snips so he could get two fingers in the opening, then pulled them out. Between his index and middle fingers was a flat piece of metal, slightly larger than a quarter. He dropped it into his palm. It pulsed with light. And the handbag slowly stopped glowing.

"Do you have any idea what it is?" Ruthie asked, astonished by what she was seeing.

It was nothing at all like Christina's key, no elaborate metalwork. The metal looked cheap, and the design was very plain. Scuffed and scratched, it was roughly a square, with letters and numbers stamped into it on the diagonal. A hole had been punched at one of the corners. If she had come across it on the ground, it wouldn't have looked like anything of value—except for the fact that it was glowing.

"What does that say?" Ruthie asked. It was hard to make out because the metal was so worn. "It looks like *C-h-a-r* something. And then some numbers—*587*. And some more letters—something *v-a-n-t, 1835*. What is it?"

"Beats me; kind of looks like a really beat-up pet license or a soldier's dog tag." Jack shook his head. "But I think you have to try touching it."

Ruthie looked around first to make sure no one was near, then he handed it to her. The moment she touched it, the glow from the odd object increased, the warmth spreading just like the key. The neckline of her T-shirt began to feel loose, and the process that was now so familiar to Ruthie began.

Before she had shrunk even an inch, she dropped it right back in Jack's palm, and brushed away the hair that had suddenly blown in her face. As soon as Jack got past the surprise of what had just started to happen, he smiled. "We'll get to warn Louisa after all," he said.

Ruthie felt overwhelmingly relieved. "I hope it works like the key works and you'll shrink with me."

"Only one way to find out," Jack responded.

They went back into the gallery, which was beginning to feel crowded, and stood near the door to the corridor.

"Is it my imagination, or is that guard over there watching us?" Jack whispered.

Ruthie shot a glance in that direction. "Let's just go over here for a few minutes to be safe," she said, walking away from the alcove toward the American rooms. They were directly in front of room A1, the room from Massachusetts at the time of the Salem witch trials.

As she looked at the room Ruthie felt a jolt. "Do you see what I see? Or don't see?" she asked.

"I don't know—what?"

"Thomas' *Mayflower*! It's gone!"

"Maybe it's been moved."

They looked, but they didn't see it anywhere.

"First the globe. Now the *Mayflower*," Ruthie said. "I wonder what else is missing."

"This just gets weirder and weirder," Jack said.

A large family moved slowly through the gallery. Finally Ruthie motioned to Jack to walk back to the door. One more quick check around them and then Jack put the metal square in her palm, sandwiching the magic piece of metal between their hands. Ruthie felt the heat against her skin. The breeze came up, and the shrinking started. But she felt somehow different, almost stiff, like on some cold mornings when you've just gotten out of bed. She looked up to observe the alcove ceiling zooming way out as though expanding to sky height. And then it stopped!

Jack and Ruthie looked at each other; they were no longer shrinking but still stood about a foot tall, not five inches—far too big to get under the door, and way too visible! In those couple of seconds only half thoughts could form in Ruthie's brain, but one thing was clear to her: *We aren't small enough!*

Ruthie was about to do the only thing she could think to do: drop the metal square. But then—like an engine starting up again after a stall—the room began to swirl and continued to grow around them, stopping when they stood five inches tall. They hit the lumpy carpet and darted under the door just as a couple of kids came around the corner.

"Did you see that?" they heard a young boy say. "I saw some kind of really big bug just go under that door!"

"We barely made it," Jack said. "This thing's magic doesn't work as fast as the key's."

"Maybe it's just because it hasn't been used in a long time," Ruthie speculated.

"Yeah, maybe. Do you think anyone saw us shrink?"

"I'm not sure—I don't think so," Ruthie said, uncertain. "Let's move down the corridor a ways before we get big again, just in case."

The miniature Ruthie and Jack traveled along the corridor on their way to E27—Louisa's room as they now thought of it. They passed two turns, then stopped dead in their tracks when, behind them, they heard the sound of the door being unlocked.

"Run!" Jack whispered. They scurried like frightened mice, hugging the baseboards. They didn't stop until they were at the end of the corridor, under the Japanese room. Then they heard footsteps followed by voices. They could just barely make out what was being said.

"Right here, that one up there," a female voice said.

"That's Dora's voice!" Ruthie held her breath reflexively.

"These bulbs are always dying," a male voice said. "Thanks for pointing it out."

They heard the sound of some metal clanking and Dora talking to the man, who they judged was a maintenance worker changing a lightbulb.

"Would you mind leaving your stepladder here for a little while?" they heard Dora asking. "I'm taking a few notes and there's nothing to sit on. This would be perfect."

"Sure thing, ma'am," the man agreed. "Just let one of us know when you're all finished with it."

"Thank you so much," she said.

Then came the sound of the door opening and closing again. Ruthie looked at Jack and whispered, "Do you think they're gone?"

"Let's look."

Ruthie tiptoed, even though part of her realized it was silly, since their tiny footsteps would be impossible for anyone to hear. Jack followed. Staying close to the wall, they peeked around each corner because they weren't sure how far into the corridor Dora had come.

They made the last turn and saw the stepladder. Dora

was nowhere to be seen. They could see the door firmly closed at the end of the corridor. It appeared that she had left, leaving the ladder for another time, perhaps. But they had no idea when that might be: tomorrow, the next day, or in five minutes.

"Let's go find Louisa," Jack said without any hesitation.

"But what if Dora comes back?"

"It doesn't matter," Jack replied.

"You're right." But Ruthie couldn't shake the unease. It was something about how Dora had insisted the stepladder be left. She was trying to follow Mrs. McVittie's instruction about observing, and she told herself to remember this.

They decided it would be quicker to be big again, since Louisa's room was near the other end of the corridor. Jack took the metal square out of his pocket.

He held out his hand, the square in his palm. Luckily, this time the process seemed faster, with no stopping or slowing in the middle. Perhaps the thing was just getting warmed up.

At E27, Ruthie reached into her bag, lifted out the string ladder, and hung it from the ledge. "I've got the clothes in here too." She pulled out the tightly folded dress for her and the shirt and pants for Jack. They turned their backs to change, not facing each other until they both said, "Ready."

Ruthie looked at Jack and was surprised at how the 1930s clothing changed him.

Jack looked at Ruthie and said, "Weird!"

"Our shoes are all wrong. I couldn't fit the vintage ones in my messenger bag," Ruthie said.

"We'll just say they're what everyone in America wears," Jack advised. "If anyone cares. Let's get small."

They held hands, and Jack put the square in her free one. The breeze began, their new "old" clothes adjusted, and they shrank even more smoothly, more like with Christina's key. The magic in the square seemed fully awakened now.

They scampered up the ladder and climbed onto the ledge. Peering around the framework, they could see the roof garden of the beautiful Parisian library. No one in the gallery was looking at that moment, so they dashed across the room and out the door to the balcony. They flew down and around the spiral staircase, barely making contact with the steps. In no time they were out on the sidewalks of Paris.

Except for their sneakers, Ruthie and Jack looked as if they belonged among the Parisians of 1937. The streets were filled with people, just as they had been the last time, only now the two barely took note, wanting to find Louisa as fast as they could. They made their way quickly to the Jardins du Trocadéro and down the broad steps, and then they took a right turn to find Louisa's street, rue Le Tasse.

"Do you remember the address?" Jack asked.

"I'm pretty sure it was number seven. And she said it was the second from the end," Ruthie answered.

They passed eight or nine doorways, each of beautifully carved wood. They were all quite large and most had big, round brass knobs centered right in the middle, nothing like American front doors. Every door was unique; some had fine carvings, others were rather plain. They came to number seven and saw the metal nameplate next to a door buzzer.

"There it is—'Meyer, fourth floor,'" Ruthie read. Jack lifted his finger to push, but Ruthie grabbed his arm. "Wait—we haven't even planned what we're going to say to them."

Jack shrugged. "Easy. We'll say our dad is a businessman—"

"What kind of businessman?" Ruthie interrupted.

"Import-export," he said off the top of his head.

"What's that?"

"It's exactly what it sounds like; buying and selling stuff from different countries. I'm sure it will work. Anyway, we'll tell them our dad talks to important businesspeople all over the world. We'll say that when we told him we met Louisa in the park the other day, he said he hoped they weren't planning on staying in Paris, that Jewish people need to go to England or the United States as soon as they can to be safe from the Nazis. Simple."

"What if they don't believe us?"

"If we don't ring this doorbell, we'll never find out if they believe us or not." He pushed the button.

They waited. Jack pushed the button once more. No

answer. And then a third time. Neither one of them had considered the possibility that no one would be home.

Just then, a woman leaned out of the ground-floor window right next to where they were standing. She was a rough-looking woman, her weathered face a stark contrast to the white lace curtains and red geraniums in the window boxes that framed her.

"Vous cherchez quelqu'un?" the woman said brusquely. Ruthie froze as Jack looked at her for a response.

"Répétez, s'il vous plaît." Ruthie figured asking the woman to repeat herself would at least buy her some time.

The woman said it again, barely any slower but definitely louder. Ruthie's brain kicked in and she smiled.

"Nous cherchons la famille Meyer, s'il vous plaît." Turning to Jack, she translated, "We're looking for the Meyer family."

"La famille Meyer n'est pas ici!" the woman said harshly.

"They're not here?" Ruthie repeated in English. Then she quickly tried to ask in French where they were. *"Où sont-ils?"*

"À la campagne. Ils reviendront vendredi."

"What'd she say?" Jack asked.

"They're in the country. And something about Friday, I think." Ruthie really wasn't certain. *"Vendredi?"* she asked the woman again.

"Oui! J'ai dit vendredi," the woman said, and blew air through her lips as she shooed them away like flies.

"You don't have to know French to figure out she

wasn't being friendly," Jack commented when the woman had disappeared behind the curtains. They heard the sound of a radio coming from inside, getting louder as if telling them to leave. "So what do you think she said?"

"I'm pretty sure—but not positive—she said the Meyer family has gone to the country and will be back Friday." Ruthie let out a big sigh.

This mission was weighing on her. It felt like such a huge responsibility, and she wanted to know that she had done her job and that Louisa would be safe.

"Hey, we'll just come back Saturday, then," he said, eternally optimistic. "We're going to that big gala thing with my mom. We can sneak in then."

"But are we sure it will be Saturday here?" Ruthie questioned.

"When we went back to visit Sophie, the time had passed the same as our time. Remember?" Jack reasoned.

"True."

"Besides, we don't have any other choice, do we?"

··· 9 ···
PHOEBE

JACK CHECKED HIS WATCH. "MY mom isn't expecting us until dinner. We've still got plenty of time to check out the South Carolina room to see if the handbag really comes from there."

"While we're on the American side, let's go see if we can find out anything about where Thomas' *Mayflower* might be. You know, like Mrs. McVittie told us to do—look again and find clues," Ruthie suggested.

As they retraced their steps along the streets of Paris, Ruthie observed that many of the windows had well-tended flower boxes. Shops had beautifully lettered signs with pictures describing what kind of business it was: bakery signs showed cakes, others displayed paintings of yummy-looking cheese, or elegant shoes and hats. Paris seemed like a wonderful place to live, with all the people strolling on the broad sidewalks and enjoying themselves in sidewalk cafés and restaurants. She thought how awful it must have felt when the Nazis occupied the city and how horrible it would have been if they'd never been driven out. Could something like that ever happen in her life, in Chicago? She couldn't imagine it; it was unthinkable.

They hiked up the spiral staircase and in no time were back in the corridor and leaping from the ledge. At their full size, they rolled up the ladder and stuffed it in Ruthie's bag. They found their clothes right where they had left them and changed again before heading toward the duct-tape climbing strip.

The strip allowed them to reach the air vent leading to the duct that ran above the ceiling, over the viewing space. They could pass through it to get to the access corridor for the American rooms. The vent measured roughly two feet wide by ten inches tall, so they had to be small to fit. It was also about eight feet from the ground, which didn't seem so high when they were full-sized. But when they were small, the scale change was daunting—it was like climbing a nine-story building. Ruthie marveled with pride at her creation, with its two strips of tape securing the middle one, which had the adhesive side out. At the base of the strip, Jack held Ruthie's hand, the metal square between their palms, and they shrank. The climb was incredibly long, but it was the only way.

Ruthie shifted her messenger bag so that it sat squarely on her back, and she started climbing by pressing her hands to the sticky path. Then she lifted her toes to the strip. She hadn't forgotten how to do it: release only one hand or foot at a time for stability. Left hand, right hand, left foot, right foot, over and over. Jack followed behind her. She was surprised at how well they both clambered up the wall, as if they did it every day.

The climbing strip was still in good condition, but it had picked up a layer of dust, which to their tiny hands felt pretty chunky, like bread crumbs. Hand over hand they neared the top. When they were just about at the air vent, they heard the distinct sound of the key in the lock.

"Quick, into the vent!" Jack directed. Ruthie was already doing just that. They lay flat on their stomachs, peering over the edge into the immense space below. They saw two men in maintenance clothes, one carrying a toolbox, walking in their direction. The two climbers knew they were in trouble.

"It's somewhere along here, near a vent," one man said. "Look, here it is."

The two men were standing directly below them, inspecting the three strips of duct tape. One man scratched his head.

"Well, that's the darnedest thing. Can't imagine what it's for." Their eyes followed the strips from the floor all the way up to the vent. Ruthie and Jack withdrew out of sight.

Opening the toolbox, the men pulled out two flat-edged scrapers, using them to pry the tape from the wall. "Gonna take some time," one said as they began dismantling the only escape route Ruthie and Jack had.

They crawled farther into the darkness of the vent. "That's not good," Jack whispered.

"Let's just hope they haven't been in the American corridor yet and taken down our climbing strip on that side," Ruthie whispered back.

"We'll have to jump if it's gone."

Ruthie groaned, remembering how hard they had hit the floor the last time they'd had to do that. "Might as well keep going." She stood up. "Do you have your flashlight?"

"Didn't bring it this time. Are you okay?"

"Yeah," Ruthie answered. The complete darkness made them feel even smaller as they headed into it. The first time they'd made this trek they'd been knocked flat by a gust of hot air, so they were prepared when it happened again—though this time the air was cool from the air-conditioning. They heard the rumble just before it hit them, and they crouched low. With the chilled wind at their backs, they proceeded.

About a hundred paces along they began to see faint light coming from the American rooms. They picked up speed and finally arrived at the edge. They dropped to their hands and knees and felt for the adhesive.

"It's still there!" Jack said. "Ready to climb down?"

"Ready," Ruthie responded.

Jack went first. "Ew," he said halfway down. Not only had dust gotten stuck on the adhesive, but a couple of flies had alighted on the sticky surface and never escaped. They measured about the length of Ruthie's forearm.

Such close-ups of dead insects were something Ruthie and Jack hadn't expected. The prickly hairs covering the inert creatures were stiff and spiky, the eyes—with their hundreds of individual globes—appeared fake, and their jointed legs looked more like mechanical inventions.

"But the wings are kind of beautiful," Ruthie commented, wondering if one of them was the fly she had freed last time.

Now on the ledge, Jack suggested they go to Thomas' room first. They hustled along the narrow path, stopping at A1 and the entrance to the side room, the one with the two low beds.

"Look around—do you see the ship anywhere?" Jack asked.

There weren't many possible places for it to be, but they checked thoroughly, including under the beds and in a small chest. Then they peered around the corner into the main room. The ship was not visible; when they had the chance, they entered the room and opened the doors of the cabinet. It was empty. They checked behind the high-back bench and then exited into the entryway that led to the outdoors—and the seventeenth century. It wasn't in this room either. Ruthie felt tempted to go out looking for Thomas. But then she noticed something.

"Jack, look." She was standing at the door, looking out its window. "It's not alive anymore." Jack joined her. They saw a painted diorama, not the dusty street where they'd been chased by a witch-hunting mob. They looked up and even saw a lightbulb creating the daylight. "It's like the Japanese garden."

"I wonder why." They stared at the lifeless diorama. "Maybe the square isn't bringing it to life?" Jack theorized.

"I don't know. It worked in the Paris room—if it was the metal square making that happen." She looked around, breathing the stuffy air. "I think it's something else. Remember when we read in the archives what Mrs. Thorne said about objects animating the rooms? And remember my dad told us *animating* can mean 'bringing things to life'?"

"The *Mayflower*," Jack said, understanding what she meant.

"Exactly. Maybe the really old objects—like the *Mayflower* and Sophie's journal—are what make these rooms time portals. It must be! Without the *Mayflower* in the room, the outside isn't alive."

"And Mrs. Thorne must have known."

"Or at least one of her craftsmen," Ruthie suggested.

"I'll add that to the rules list: that something really old in the rooms animates the dioramas," Jack noted.

"I wonder where the ship is." Ruthie scanned the room.

"It's not here," Jack declared. "That's for sure."

"And without the *Mayflower* in the room," Ruthie observed, "it's like an entire world's been stolen."

. . .

Entering room A29, the South Carolina ballroom, was tricky. They had to use a side door, which was completely closed, so they couldn't tell if anyone was looking at the room or not. They put their ears to the door, but that didn't really help.

The door obviously hadn't been opened for a long time—maybe not since Mrs. McVittie and her sister had visited—and the knob felt stiff and squeaked as it turned. Ruthie gave it a nudge and immediately heard a voice from the museum. She froze with the door open a few inches.

"Did you see that door move just now?" The voice sounded like that of an older woman.

An older man's voice said, "I didn't see anything. Maybe the air-conditioning went on and there's a bit of airflow in there."

"You're probably right," the first voice responded.

From where they stood, Ruthie and Jack could see reflections in an oval mirror hanging on the opposite wall. It caught the tops of heads as they passed by. Watching the mirror, they waited for their moment to go in.

Once inside, Ruthie was surprised by how small the space was; since it was called a ballroom, she expected it to feel larger. At the far end she saw an elaborately decorated piano, next to a graceful harp and another instrument that looked like a lyre (she'd seen one of those when they studied ancient Greece in school). A plump sofa covered in green silk sat beside the fireplace. Ruthie walked over to a tall wood cabinet with gold trim, near the front of the room. Behind the panes of glass the doors were curtained, hiding whatever rested on its shelves. She felt an overwhelming impulse to open it.

A few chairs anchoring the corners of the rug had colors and designs that corresponded to the handbag. The handbag! She opened her messenger bag to check on it. Sure enough, the gems were faintly pulsing with light—not as bright as when the metal square had been hidden within the lining, but still, it was unnaturally bright. Since the metal square was in her pocket, Ruthie wondered, what was making it glow? She was about to reach into her pocket to see if the square showed any signs of warmth when Jack grabbed her arm.

"Uh-oh!" he pulled her across the room to a set of open French doors that led to a side porch. They hurried out just as three kids came into view through the glass.

They found themselves standing on a grand covered porch, painted white. Though the air was still and thick—much hotter than Chicago—the sounds of birds, voices, and other street noises couldn't be missed. This world was alive!

They climbed the steps down from the porch and came to what looked like a freestanding front door facing the street. Neither of them had ever seen a front door that opened to a porch instead of into a house. Next to it an ornate wrought iron fence enclosed them in a very large garden adjacent to the house.

"Where are we?" Jack asked.

"Charleston, South Carolina, I'm pretty sure. That's what the catalogue said. I think before 1835."

"Cool. That's before the Civil War." Jack looked up and down the street. From where they stood, they had an expansive corner view of an intersection. It looked nothing like Chicago—from any time. "Look—palm trees!"

Besides palm trees, Ruthie and Jack saw a bustling town, with horse-drawn carts and carriages, gracious homes mostly painted white, and quite a large number of people going about their day. The women were wearing dresses with huge ruffled skirts and elaborate necklines, and bonnets on their heads. The men were wearing something like tuxedos. No one seemed to be dressed simply, despite the heat. Ruthie wanted to explore but realized that they would stand out too much in their modern clothes.

"If this is before the Civil War, do you think some of these people are slaves?" she asked Jack, noticing the large proportion of African American faces.

"I guess so," Jack said. They saw dark-skinned people driving the carriages that light-skinned people were riding in. But they also saw a few people who might have been slaves who appeared to be selling goods from street corner stalls, such as handmade baskets with beautiful striped patterns.

Ruthie turned to look away from the street and into the garden in which they stood. "I wonder how far this garden goes," she said, and began to walk along a brick path lined with flowers and herbs. On the far end to one side, beyond some huge oak trees, stood two more structures that looked very much like the facade of the ballroom. In between, there was no grassy lawn; the entire area was lushly planted with aromatic flowers and shrubs. The rich and heavy smells had an intensity that was not familiar to Ruthie. They came across a rose garden, a small landscaped maze, and another area with a small fountain and benches. It was as though the outdoors had been designed with separate rooms, just like the interior of a house, all perfectly weeded and not a leaf out of place.

"This is so pretty," Ruthie said.

"Thank you, ma'am," a voice answered.

Startled, Jack and Ruthie spun around and found themselves face to face with a girl who looked to be almost their age. She had dark skin, her hair was braided in tight, even rows, and she was wearing plainer clothes than what they had seen on the people in the street. A dull brown dress that stopped just above her ankles and had a high collar was covered by a loose-fitting jumper—like an apron—made in a well-worn calico print. The girl held a large watering can. "You visiting the Smith family?" she continued, her expression a combination of curiosity and wariness. She spoke with a thick southern accent.

"Yes, that's right," Jack said immediately. "I'm Jack and this is Ruthie. We're here from Chicago."

"That up north?" the girl asked.

"Yes," Ruthie answered. "But we're not staying here for long. Just passing through."

"Those traveling clothes?" The girl looked them up and down, especially their shoes.

"Yes," Jack replied. "What's your name?"

The girl appeared surprised by the question and stared at Jack for a moment before responding, "I'm Phoebe."

"This sure is a beautiful garden." Jack looked around at the greenery. "Do you work here?"

"Yes, I do. With my father. He's in charge out here. We're with the Gillis family." Phoebe nodded to the grand house at the far end of the garden. "My mother works inside, and next year I will too."

"Doing what?" Ruthie asked.

"Serving, of course!" Phoebe answered as though it were the silliest question she'd ever heard.

"We don't live with servants in Chicago." Ruthie hoped that might explain her question.

"Where do they live?" Phoebe asked.

"Ruthie means we don't have servants at all," Jack explained.

"Oh. I've heard about that. About up north." She made "up north" sound like it was another planet. She shook her head the way people do when they hear something unimaginable. "How do people get on?"

"We get on just fine," Ruthie answered, although she was not at all sure what Phoebe meant by the question.

Was she asking how people got along with each other, or how they functioned on a daily basis without slaves?

Just then Phoebe's eyes widened and she said, "Quick, follow me." She led them around a large flowering bush to a shed nestled in an out-of-the-way corner. "In here." She opened the door and motioned for them to enter. It was a potting shed, neatly organized with gardening tools hanging from nails on the wall. A small window over a worktable let in light. "We'll wait in here for a spot."

"Why? What for?" Jack asked.

"You didn't hear him? James Gillis?" Phoebe asked.

"I didn't hear anyone," Ruthie answered.

"Neither did I," Jack said.

"Maybe my ears are just listenin' for him 'cuz he's always callin' for me. Soon as I get started on something, he wants me to do something else. He's always interruptin'," she explained. "You'd think he was master around here!"

"Who is he?" Ruthie asked.

"He is Master Gillis' last son. He's younger than me! Not yet eight even! But really I belong to his older brother, Martin."

Ruthie had read a little about slavery in history class; still, this last statement amazed her. "What do you mean?"

"Master Gillis gave me to Master Martin last year. But he's away in college and only needed one servant, so I stayed here. You sure you don't have servants in . . . where was it?"

"Chicago," Ruthie answered. "No, we don't."

"I've heard stories . . . some folks save enough money to buy their freedom and head up north." She thought for a minute. "Do you think I'd like Chicago?"

"Sure," Jack said. "It's colder, though, and we don't have palm trees."

"Do you go to school in Chicago?" she asked.

"Yes," Jack said.

"Even you?" Phoebe asked Ruthie.

"Yes. We go to the same school."

Phoebe shook her head again in disbelief. "I think I'd like to try going to school. Can you keep a secret?"

"Of course," Ruthie responded as she and Jack nodded.

"I can read. And write some. Look," she said eagerly, pulling a book from a pocket under her apron. It was a much-used copy of *A Little Pretty Pocket-Book*, by John Newbery. Ruthie and Jack could see it was a book of rhymes illustrated with simple woodcuts.

Phoebe proudly pointed out her name written on the inside cover. "I don't understand all of it, but I can read most of the words."

"Why is it a secret?" Ruthie wanted to know.

Phoebe answered cautiously, "Folks don't like their servants reading. You won't tell?"

"Never!" Ruthie promised.

"And you?" Phoebe eyed Jack with a look that meant business.

"Promise!" he replied.

"All right, then," she said, softening.

Jack was about to say something when they too heard the insistent voice of a boy—James Gillis—calling out for Phoebe.

"Just when I'm in the middle of something," she said.

"What were you in the middle of doing?" Jack asked.

Phoebe looked at him like he was dim-witted. "Why, I was having the nicest conversation with you! Remember?"

"You said you worked with your father. Doing what?" Ruthie asked.

"The herb garden. Maybe you walked by?" She beamed. "That's mine. I know all about herbs for cookin' and elixirs for curin'."

"Curing?" Jack asked.

"You know, medicines, preparations. My grandmother taught me, and now it's my job." She turned to Ruthie. "He doesn't know much, does he?"

"Not about that." Ruthie smiled. "Do you get to practice your reading and writing very much?"

"Readin' is easy to practice. I have this book—and there's others in the house that I . . . uh . . . borrow. I always put them back. James Gillis is supposed to be readin', but he doesn't take to it much. Writin' is harder to practice, because I don't have a slate of my own."

Then Ruthie had an idea. She reached into her messenger bag and pulled out her small spiral-bound notebook. She tore out the few pages that had writing on them and shoved those back in the bag. "Here. Why don't you keep this," Ruthie offered.

Phoebe's mouth fell open. "For me? A book of paper? And it's got the lines already on it so I can keep straight!" She turned to see how many empty pages there were. "You can do without this?"

Jack jumped in. "She can get another one." Then he nudged Ruthie. "Don't you have some pencils in there too?"

Ruthie sank her hand in and rummaged around, finding two pencils.

Phoebe grinned from ear to ear and immediately wrote her name on the first page. "Thank you, Ruthie. This is just what I've been needin'. Now I can practice my writin'!"

"You're welcome."

"May I ask a favor?" Phoebe seemed hesitant.

"Sure," Ruthie said.

"Would you write that this is a gift from you to me, so people know that's the truth?"

"Of course." Phoebe handed her the notebook and one of the pencils, and Ruthie printed *A gift to Phoebe, from Ruthie Stewart* on the cover. Ruthie passed it back. "How's that?"

"That's real good. Thank you. Now I best be gettin' on. I don't want a beatin'," she said, so matter-of-factly it gave Ruthie chills. Phoebe opened the door a crack and looked out first. "You wait in here and come out after me. I don't want James to know I's talkin' to you."

"Okay," Ruthie said.

Phoebe turned and looked puzzled. "What does that mean?" she asked.

Jack and Ruthie simultaneously remembered Thomas' mother asking the same thing! "It means 'all right,'" Ruthie explained. "In Chicago."

After the door closed behind the young girl, Ruthie looked at Jack, stunned. "We just met someone who is owned by someone else!"

"It's pretty unbelievable," Jack responded. "Imagine what it must be like for her."

Ruthie was quiet for a minute. "It's hard, isn't it—to imagine, I mean."

"I wonder what will—what did happen to her," Jack said.

Ruthie found it difficult to contemplate. There were too many bad options. Just like Louisa, Phoebe was caught in a circumstance that was totally unfair and filled with danger. Both these girls' lives were filled with cruelty and pain simply because they had been born in a certain place and time.

"We should probably get out of here before anyone finds us. I don't want to cause trouble for her."

"Neither do I." Ruthie opened the door of the shed an inch and listened. They heard what must surely have been young James Gillis giving orders, his voice that of a high-pitched tyrant. They waited until the sound moved farther away. When it was all quiet they left the shed.

Carefully, so they wouldn't be seen, they made their way through the garden back to the porch steps. Ruthie had realized that, just as had happened before, only people experiencing the magic could see the entrances to the rooms. To anyone else, the garden appeared to continue on. From Ruthie and Jack's point of view, it was like being in two worlds at once: seeing the garden and the nineteenth century in front of them, and seeing the Thorne Room and today just behind them.

They waited outside the French doors for a while, to make sure they had a clear opportunity to reenter the room. As they stood there, they saw James Gillis wending his way along one of the garden paths, coming very close to the porch. He looked directly at them but through them, a bored look on his face. Soon he saw something that caught his attention: an anthill in the cracks of the brick path. He bent down to investigate. Then, like a true tormentor, he proceeded to stomp on the ants as they scattered, not stopping until he had squashed every last one.

Racing across the room, they ran to the door through which they had entered. Ruthie made sure to leave it ajar.

"I almost forgot," Ruthie said as they stopped on the ledge. "When we came through the room the first time, I checked the handbag. It was definitely glowing, especially when I was standing close to that tall cabinet."

"You think that means something?"

"I don't know. Maybe. I'd really like to—" Ruthie was about to say she wanted to run in and take a look but was interrupted by the sound of the PA system announcing that the museum would be closing in ten minutes.

Jack looked at his watch. "Wait—what day is it?"

"Wednesday."

Jack slapped his palm to his forehead. "I thought today was Thursday, when the museum closes at eight!"

"We don't have time to climb back to the other corridor." Ruthie knew she should have been paying attention to the time. There was only one possible way out. "We'll have to go out through that access door full-sized!" They had tried fitting under before and found there was no gap between the bottom of the door and the carpet on this side to crawl under; it was the reason they'd built the climbing strip in the first place.

"It's right in front of the information booth. This could be worse than not good," Jack said, though he didn't sound nearly as worried as Ruthie felt. What if they got caught sneaking out through the door with a stolen Art Institute key in their hands? What if they didn't find a chance to sneak out until after the museum closed and they got picked up by security cameras? Ruthie's heart throbbed faster and faster in her ears.

They followed the ledge until it ended at the door that would lead them back to Gallery 11, directly in front of the entrance and the information desk, where a guard almost always stood. They would have to wait until everyone had cleared out of the museum, but not too long after. Timing was everything.

"Ready to get big?" Jack calmly asked.

"Do we have a choice?"

Ruthie took the metal square from her pocket and grabbed his hand. She let the square drop and they stepped into thin air. The space shrank around them and their full-sized feet hit the ground just as they heard another announcement: "The museum is now closed."

Jack put the square in his pocket, reaching in another pocket for the Art Institute key. He looked at his watch. "We'll wait three minutes."

"Can you hear anyone?" she asked.

Jack put his ear to the door and listened. "Nope."

"Keep listening," Ruthie said, feeling the eternity of the wait. She decided to look in her messenger bag to see what, if anything, was happening with the beaded bag. The rhinestones appeared dull and quiet; maybe a few tiny glints, but nothing like what she had seen in the room. She had a hunch there must be something in that cabinet behind its drawn curtains. But what?

Jack put his finger to his lips in a quiet sign. He slipped the Art Institute key into the lock and turned it slowly. He waited a few beats, then gently but firmly pushed the door open. They heard nothing—no footsteps, no voices. Jack slipped out; Ruthie, barely breathing, followed right behind him. The door closed and locked.

"Okay. No problem. Now just look normal," he whispered. Ruthie doubted she could carry that off at the moment. All was fine until they were climbing the staircase to the main floor and a guard approached them coming down.

"What are you doing here? The museum is closed," he said sharply, hands on hips.

"I had to wait for her," Jack explained. "She doesn't feel so good and was in the bathroom."

The guard looked at Ruthie. In fact, she did look sick to her stomach, so the guard bought Jack's excuse. "You'd better hurry to the main entrance." He continued down the staircase.

Jack smiled at Ruthie. "Good performance."

"Not acting," she replied.

··· 10 ···
A FUNNY COINCIDENCE

WHILE JACK WAS BUSY ON his computer and Lydia made dinner, Ruthie stood in Lydia's studio admiring one of her canvases. It was a study for the large trompe l'oeil mural Dora had commissioned her to paint. This one showed a deep landscape with an old building in the foreground. It looked as if Ruthie could reach right into it.

"What do you think?" Lydia asked, coming around the corner.

"How do you do it? It looks so real!" Ruthie asked.

"Trompe l'oeil relies on perspective. Has Dora taught you that yet?"

"Yes, but I still can't make it look like yours."

"It takes a lot of practice. It also takes some tricks of perception. After all, *trompe l'oeil* is French for 'fool the eye.'"

Ruthie tilted her head, pondering how her eyes were being tricked.

"Think about it," Lydia went on. "You're trying to create a three-dimensional image on a flat surface. It's an illusion, that's all. Does that make sense?"

"I suppose so. But the more I think about it, the more complicated it gets!"

"It can be," Lydia agreed, "and things aren't always as they seem, are they?"

"That's like what Mrs. McVittie said to me—that I should question assumptions."

"That's good advice. It works for all kinds of things, including visual assumptions. Try to apply it when you're practicing your sketches. Sometimes your eyes see one thing, but your brain convinces you it's something else."

The phone rang, and Lydia stepped away to answer it. After she'd hung up, she returned to the kitchen. "Soup's on," she called.

"Who was on the phone?" Jack skidded to the table.

"A friend of mine with good news about the art thefts. It seems they've caught the thief." Lydia handed Jack silverware to set next to big soup bowls on the table.

"What happened?" Ruthie asked.

"Apparently the police received information from a former girlfriend of a guy who worked part-time for a catering company that did business with many of the people whose art has been stolen. This young woman was suspicious when the guy gave her a necklace that he couldn't possibly afford. And then he told her that the necklace was a tip from a catering job at one of the homes that had been robbed. She didn't believe him, so she went to the police. He'd had some minor trouble with the police before this. They found his fingerprints in the residences that were hit." Lydia ladled tortilla soup into big bowls, adding avocado and Mexican cheese on top.

"How many thefts were there altogether?" Ruthie wanted to know.

"About a dozen have been reported."

"Did they get the art back?" Jack asked.

"I'm not sure. That could take some time, especially if he sold it on the black market already. But they have enough evidence to keep him in custody."

"You know people who've had stuff stolen, right, Mom?"

"Yes. In fact, a residence I'm working in right now was robbed," she replied. "Others are collectors who are well known and socially active. You know, people who host fund-raising parties, or open their homes to celebrate young artists in their collections. So I know who they are, but I don't really know them. People are sure going to be relieved when this news gets out."

Lydia's dinner was so delicious, Ruthie ate as much as Jack. Afterward, Ruthie asked if she could see photos of more of Lydia's trompe l'oeil murals. Lydia opened a file on her computer. "I took these photos the other day."

"It's beautiful," Ruthie said admiringly. She saw an elegant entry hall with a black-and-white marble floor and a curving staircase. On one side, the floor appeared to continue into another room, this one with a view of the Swiss Alps. Anyone standing there would be persuaded the majestic mountains could be seen out the window—from an apartment in the middle of Chicago!

"The family is Swiss; they miss the Alps, so I painted them. And then they redecorated the whole apartment to feel like Switzerland. Dora Pommeroy was their decorator," Lydia explained.

"Weird," Jack said, studying the computer screen. He walked over to his mother's drawing table and picked something up. It was a photo of the room where she was planning her newest mural. Holding it next to the screen, he pointed first to a detail in the photograph, then to a detail in the computer image. "Why are there single green apples on tables in both of these pictures? Did you put them there, Mom?"

"No, I didn't. I actually didn't even notice them when I was there." Lydia looked back and forth from her computer screen to the printed photo. "What a funny coincidence."

But then Ruthie noticed something that made the tortilla soup roil horribly in her stomach. In the photo Jack held she saw not only a green apple—she saw a globe!

When they went back into Jack's room to collect her messenger bag, Ruthie quickly told Jack that the globe in the photo looked identical to the one missing from the Thorne Rooms, but they couldn't really talk with his mom around. By the time Lydia and Jack dropped Ruthie off, Mrs. McVittie was already in her nightgown and dozing in her chair, so Ruthie couldn't bring up the subject with her.

She put on her pajamas and climbed into bed with Mrs. McVittie's copy of the catalogue, hoping to see that the globe looked somehow different from the one in Lydia's photo. She paged through the book, telling herself she must be mistaken. But there on the desk in room E6 sat the two old globes on their wooden tripod stands. There was no denying it: they were identical to the one in the photo, except, of course, they were much smaller.

Ruthie tried to sleep, but what kept running through her mind was the awful notion that Dora might have something to do with the globe being in that apartment. All she knew for certain was what Lydia had told her: that the family had hired Dora to redecorate. Maybe it was just a standard type of antique globe, or a replica. Probably decorators had copies made all the time, she thought. And there were so many other people who also had access to the Thorne Rooms and could have taken the newly missing items. Ruthie knew from the archive curator that things had to be removed from the rooms to be repaired, such as when the old glue dried out or delicate threads broke because of age.

Wasn't assuming that Dora had taken the globe the sort of assumption that Mrs. McVittie had told her to question? Or was it the other way around: should she assume Dora was innocent? Ruthie was completely confused and beginning to feel guilty for having such negative thoughts about Dora. She had been so generous to find time to give Ruthie the drawing lessons. And, after all, Lydia said Dora had a great reputation.

But the possibility snowballed in her head, crowding all other thoughts out of the way. Even though she was having a great time staying with Mrs. McVittie, and even though she couldn't talk to them about this dilemma, right now she missed her mom and dad. Especially her dad; she would give anything for a hug from him right now. It was a horrible night, but sheer exhaustion eventually brought sleep.

She was awakened by Mrs. McVittie, next to her bed, shaking her.

"Ruthie, dear, wake up. Jack is here and he's quite upset."

Ruthie cracked one eye to look at the clock. Seven forty-five. Impossible! But there was Jack, in the doorway, looking stressed out. He held his laptop.

"What's going on?" She sat up and rubbed her eyes.

"I couldn't sleep last night. Something was bugging me. And then I remembered this. Look." Jack sat down on her bed, flipped open his computer, and turned it on. He shoved a disk in the drive.

The video image on the screen was of Jack's room as seen from the tiny camera he had placed atop the door frame. On the video, a phone rang, and then Lydia's voice could be heard taking the call. After a few seconds, Dora entered and surveyed the room. She scanned his book-shelf, opened and closed a desk drawer and then kneeled down to look under his couch. She pulled out the shoe box and rummaged through it. Then, clear as day, Dora slipped Christina's key into her pocket. She was swift, assured and calm. The whole thing had taken less than three minutes.

"It must have happened when we went to buy milk, remember?" Jack explained. "So much for being trustworthy."

Ruthie felt all the breath escape from her lungs. She tried to refill them, inhaling only marginally enough air. She couldn't cry, since you need big gobs of oxygen for a good sob. Her throat had tightened like some invisible hand was choking her, and she felt the spot between her ribs caving in. Ruthie had never experienced this before, but she knew what it was: betrayal.

Mrs. McVittie put her hand on Ruthie's shoulder. "Don't worry, Ruthie. We can work this out. I'll make some breakfast for us all." She headed out of the room.

Ruthie felt an uncontrollable rumble start from deep in her stomach, radiating to her arms and legs. She was shaking all over. "Jack—" she began.

"Mrs. McVittie's right," he said, interrupting her. "Look, now we know for sure what happened to the key. We'll just get it back."

"But I trusted her!"

"Ruthie, it's not like it was a real friend who did this," Jack said.

"I feel so gullible."

"You're a kid. Grown-ups aren't supposed to trick us," he reasoned.

She was grateful he had said "trick *us*," like they were in it together.

Jack left to help Mrs. McVittie. As Ruthie got dressed, she thought how she had always expected—assumed—that the adults in her life would be good to her, would be fair. Her parents, Ms. Biddle, Lydia, Mrs. McVittie—they would never do something like this. And then she thought about Louisa and Phoebe, and about how the worlds they lived in were filled with grown-ups doing the wrong thing. Her problem with Dora was minuscule in comparison. But what if the people in charge started breaking the rules, or stopped doing the right thing? In the midst of her quivering panic (which made her want to pull the covers back over her head and stay in bed until this all went away), Ruthie also felt the beginnings of a different impulse: people like this had to be stopped, and she might have to be the one to do it.

They sat in the kitchen for a long time, Ruthie in dazed silence. Jack explained to Mrs. McVittie about the missing globe and *Mayflower*. He also remembered to tell her about the metal square they'd found inside the lining of the beaded bag.

"I wonder what it is," Mrs. McVittie said. "Where is it now?"

"It's in my backpack." Jack went to get it while Ruthie still sat quietly.

He returned with it in the palm of his hand and turned it over for Mrs. McVittie to see both sides. It wasn't quite glowing, but it certainly had an odd sheen for something so beat up.

"Hmmm. Curious indeed. I've no idea what it is."

"I thought for sure it was some kind of antique thinga-majig that you could name," Jack said.

"I'm sure you two will figure it out eventually." She turned back to flip the pancakes. "Do some research."

That was not what Ruthie wanted to hear; she wanted answers—now. But Jack and Mrs. McVittie talked over all the angles, all the possibilities of how to go forward.

"At least they caught the art thief," Jack said.

"Yes," Mrs. McVittie said. "I heard on the news last night."

Listening to their conversation and inhaling the smell of pancakes browning was soothing; Ruthie's throat finally opened up and the shaking subsided.

"What will you two do?" Mrs. McVittie asked eventually.

"We can't call the police, that's for sure," Jack said. "They'd never believe us."

Ruthie swallowed hard. Then she remembered today's scheduled drawing lesson. She really didn't want to go, but knew she couldn't avoid it. And her resolve was building: she couldn't let Dora get away with what she'd done. "This is my fault. I'll figure out how to get the key back."

.   .   .

Dora, wearing another fashionable outfit, greeted Ruthie and Jack with a friendly hello.

"We're going to Millennium Park after my lesson, so Jack came with," Ruthie explained.

"I hope you won't be bored waiting," Dora said.

"Bored?" he asked. "I'm going to explore the new wing. Text me when you're done."

Suddenly alone with Dora, Ruthie felt her chest tighten. She tried to calm herself, but as she walked down the stairs to Gallery 11, her legs threatened to buckle at any moment. So much had changed since her last lesson!

They started drawing. *I hope she doesn't see that my lines are wobbly*, Ruthie thought, attempting to steady her hand. Ironically, she was working on an American Shaker room, A18, which made it worse, because all the room's lines were so straight and clean and spare. She should have chosen a different room with curves and patterns, where her nervous lines would be camouflaged.

She considered various conversation openers—*So, Dora, have you ever taken anything out of the Thorne Rooms?* or, more directly, *Dora, I have a big problem. The key is missing*—but none of them felt right. What would Jack say?

Her pencil lead gave under her tension and snapped down to the wood.

"Your lead break?" Dora asked from two rooms down. "No problem. I have my sharpener. It's in my bag, in the inside pocket. Go ahead."

The large leather tote bag Dora always carried sat on the floor between the two of them. Ruthie reached down to open it and locate the inner pocket. And then it dawned on her: the key might be in it!

She peered into the deep darkness. The bag was full of the usual stuff—a phone, a small notepad, a magnifying glass, some pens, lipstick, a hairbrush—except . . . Ruthie nearly fell over when she saw what was in the very bottom of the bag: four green apples!

She stared at them for several beats.

Dora's voice entered her consciousness, sounding distorted, like a slowed-down recording. "Find it? I'm sure it's in there."

"Here it is." Ruthie's voice sounded strained even to herself.

Dora looked over at her. "Are you okay, Ruthie?"

"I don't feel well," Ruthie said, which was completely true. "I think I should find Jack and go home."

"You do look pale all of a sudden."

"Maybe I'm coming down with whatever he had," Ruthie said weakly.

"In that case, you should go home and get some rest. Let me know if you're well enough for your Saturday lesson, all right?"

"Okay, Dora. Bye." Ruthie couldn't get away from her fast enough. She left the gallery, her trembling hands trying to text Jack as she tore through the building.

Ruthie found him coming down the staircase in the new wing of the museum.

"It's pretty cool," he began, and then saw her face. "What's wrong?"

"She's—she's—the thief!" Ruthie could barely get the words out.

"I know. Wait—what do you mean?"

"Green apples . . . in her big bag."

Even though he wasn't quite sure what had happened, he understood the significance of green apples. "Let's get out of here."

They left the museum and crossed the street to Millennium Park, finding an empty bench near the *Cloud Gate* sculpture, which everyone called the Bean.

"Tell me everything," Jack said. "And breathe slowly."

Ruthie recounted how she had found the apples in the bottom of Dora's bag. "Who walks around with that many apples?"

"You're right," he agreed. "Looks like you've discovered the real art thief! And that means the police have the wrong guy in jail!"

"I should've suspected she might be the art thief when I saw the globe in the photograph. I just never thought . . . but why? Why would she steal all that stuff from all those people? And why would she leave apples when she steals something?"

"Beats me. And nobody noticed. Or at least none of

the victims mentioned it to any of the others, so nobody put it together. It's only because we saw the two photos, by chance. And then you saw the apples in her bag."

"And we saw from your video how good she is at stealing."

Ruthie and Jack sat looking at the city reflected on the curving surface of the massive silver sculpture in front of them, watching the crowds enjoying the stainless-steel Bean, endlessly fascinated by their distorted images. The rounded, mirrored surface pulled the sky so low you could touch it, and made you feel both on the ground and in the clouds. And it mirrored how Ruthie felt: unsure of what was up and what was down.

Ruthie suddenly straightened. "I just thought of something—we know Dora takes things from the rooms. Right?"

"Right."

"And without the *Mayflower* in the room, the world outside is dead, right?"

"Right."

"Jack—what if she takes something from Louisa's room, the thing that animates it? What if we can't get back to 1937 Paris to warn Louisa?"

"That would be a disaster! She hasn't done it—yet. And there are sixty-seven other rooms for her to steal from," Jack replied.

"But she might," Ruthie said. "We have to get to Louisa first!"

. . .

"Gracious! What's the matter?" Mrs. McVittie asked as they tumbled into her shop. Their faces left little doubt something had happened at Ruthie's drawing lesson. She turned the Open sign over to Closed.

They were out of breath, but Jack managed to get out one phrase: "Dora's the thief!"

"I thought we already understood that," Mrs. McVittie said.

"Not just the key. She's the art thief!" Jack declared.

"How do you know? What happened?"

"Oh, Mrs. McVittie, it was horrible," Ruthie said, and recounted everything that had led them to that conclusion. "I saw the green apples in her big bag. I'm sure it's her. But . . . why?" Ruthie paced back and forth.

"That poor, innocent man sitting in jail," Mrs. McVittie said, shaking her head. "But the issue at hand is what to do with this information."

"The apples alone won't prove anything!" Jack asserted. "And we can't tell the police we know she's the thief because she stole Christina of Milan's magic key, or that she took a tiny globe that grew to full size!"

"Jack is right," Mrs. McVittie agreed.

The midday sunlight didn't penetrate far into the shop; the yellow glow of the reading lamp encircled them instead. Ruthie felt safe in it. "We'll have to catch her red-handed," she said, not at all happy about the prospect of a confrontation. "And we have to do it fast, before she has the chance to steal something else, especially from E27!"

Jack lit up. "I got it! My camera! We can record her stealing, just like we did in my room."

"But how? Where? It's not like we know who she's going to steal from next," Ruthie said.

"A minor detail." He looked at Mrs. McVittie. "How about you?"

"Me?"

"Yeah. Why don't you hire her to redo your apartment? We can catch her stealing something."

Mrs. McVittie didn't look thrilled with the idea. "I would do it to catch a criminal, if it were absolutely necessary. . . ."

"I know!" Ruthie said suddenly. "Dr. Bell! I bet she'll help us!" After all, she explained, Caroline Bell already believed in the magic of the Thorne Rooms. Dr. Bell understood that it had to be kept a secret and—once they filled her in—would want the rooms to be protected from Dora Pommeroy.

"But what if she doesn't have anything Dora wants to steal?" Jack asked.

"I think she does," Ruthie said with confidence.

··· 11 ···
BAD APPLES

"COME IN!" DR. BELL GREETED them at her front door late Friday afternoon. "I just got home from work." Dr. Bell had returned their phone call almost immediately when they'd called the day before and she'd eagerly agreed to help. So much rested on solving this problem and solving it fast, before Dora could steal anything else. And there was no room for error in their plan.

It turned out that Dr. Bell's house needed redecorating anyway. It reminded Ruthie of her own family's apartment: comfortable but not a place where artists live. Dr. Bell was a very busy pediatrician who didn't spend much time on her house. However, unlike Ruthie's home, there were lots of interesting objects about. Dr. Bell's father had given her works of art, but she'd never figured out how to display them properly. Her collection wasn't nearly as extensive as his, but she had a few paintings and small sculptures, including some African art, and of course Edmund Bell's photographs. They not only graced the walls but leaned up against them, waiting to be hung.

"I can never decide on the best place for anything. I just don't have the knack for it," she explained to Ruthie and Jack as they looked around her living room. "And look at this," she said, picking up a small bronze geometric sculpture from a shelf. "I know it's a lovely piece, but I don't have the faintest idea where to put it." She held up another interesting object: a small African statue covered in petite white shells. "Or this. Should these two things stand next to each other like this?"

"I like your house the way it is," Ruthie offered. "It looks like you live here."

"Thank you. It does look that way, for sure." She smiled. "So tell me how you're going to work this."

Ruthie reached into her messenger bag and pulled out the silver box that Dr. Bell had given her earlier in the week, the one that belonged in room E10.

Dr. Bell's eyebrows rose when she saw it. "Is that what I think it is?"

"Yes. We haven't had a chance to put it back yet." In fact, the last time Ruthie and Jack had visited the museum, they hadn't brought it because without Christina's key they weren't even sure they'd be able to shrink. "I think this box will be useful now," Ruthie answered.

"Try it next to those two statues," Jack suggested.

"Exactly what I was thinking." Ruthie set the three objects on a small table next to the sofa. She arranged them a few times, and stood back to look at their appearance until she was satisfied with the placement.

In the meantime Jack had pulled a bunch of electronics equipment out of his backpack and was busy sorting through it all. "Let's see," he said, walking to a bookcase just across from the sofa. "This will be a good spot." From the pile of gear he picked up the small camera that had been set up over the doorway of his bedroom. He placed it with precision and removed every enticing object nearby, leaving it surrounded by paperback novels. "Let's put all your art on that side of the room."

Dr. Bell and Ruthie followed his directions while he returned to his backpack, took out his laptop and let it boot up. They finished their task and then looked on with him. He tapped a few keys on the keyboard, and a view of the room appeared on the screen.

"Voilà!" he said.

"Very impressive," Dr. Bell said.

"Let me make a few adjustments." Jack got up to change the tilt of the camera and typed a few more commands to affect the width of the angle so that the camera's view would incorporate as much of the room as possible. "There. That should do it!"

"But what about the computer?" Dr. Bell asked.

"Where's the nearest closet?" he asked.

"There's the closet in my office, right through there."
Dr. Bell pointed to a room off the living room.

"That should be good." Jack carried his laptop through
the doorway, disappearing into her office closet and closing
the door. In less than a minute he called out, "It works!
I've got a strong signal. Wave or something. Walk around."

Ruthie and Dr. Bell moved about the living room, pos-
ing for the camera from different corners. Jack reappeared.
"It's all good. I can pretty much get the entire room."

"What time did she say she'd be here?"

"Around ten," Dr. Bell answered.

"Okay. We'll get here by nine." Ruthie wondered how
her frayed nerves would make it till then.

That night Ruthie lay in bed attempting to focus on positive things and trying to picture everything going right
tomorrow. She thought about tomorrow night's gala and
what she would wear. Then she rehearsed what she and
Jack could say to Louisa when they had the chance. Ruthie
didn't allow herself to think it wouldn't happen. It had to
happen!

She put on the French tapes and luxuriated in being
alone in Mrs. McVittie's guest room as she repeated the
words aloud: *enchanté* (enchanted), *s'il vous plaît* (please),
la maison (the house), *le chien* (the dog), *une pomme* (an
apple). She drifted off to sleep.

Ruthie slept fitfully, dreaming that she was tiny, her

five-inch self stumbling over something she couldn't quite make out. Huge but indistinct shapes loomed around her. The atmosphere was foggy and out of focus. The ground beneath her was lumpy and soft, but not a nice kind of soft. She came to an edge and jumped, hoping to land on a stable surface. But just as her feet hit firmer ground the thing she had been traversing suddenly came alive and opened up as if to swallow her, like the mouth of a big black whale. And then the dark cavity came into focus; she could see it was a huge leather handbag opening menacingly in front of her. She wanted to run, but her legs felt as if they were filled with lead and wouldn't lift an inch. All at once, she heard a rumble and saw an avalanche of giant apples tumbling out of the sack, about to bury her where she stood. She raised her hands to her face in a futile attempt at self-defense.

But then, as the first apple was nearly on top of her, it shrank—they all shrank! Pounds and pounds of apples spilled out at her feet until she was standing in the middle of the pile. She picked one up, but it disappeared into thin air. She tried another, and it too vanished. These apples were not for eating, she surmised.

Ruthie wasn't sure what to do next, but the question was answered for her by a bell-like sound. It was quite faint at first but then grew loud enough for her to realize it was coming from the depths of the enormous bag. With her legs now able to move, she took a step into its blackness, the magical sound making her brave. The sound led her to Christina's key, which lay deep inside, emitting its silver-gold beacon of light. Ruthie picked it up and walked backward until she was out again. And then the gaping bag closed itself, deflating right in front of her until it was nothing but a harmless carryall.

The foggy haze that surrounded her began to clear. She still couldn't recognize much, but finally something appeared in front of her and she reached out to touch it. It was a bed—her own bed, actually, soft and comforting. It smelled of freshly washed linen. She climbed onto it and went to sleep, this time peacefully, the key safely in her hand.

Ruthie and Jack rode the bus to Dr. Bell's house in the morning, nervously checking the time because the traffic was unusually bad. They arrived at her house a little after nine, enough time to get set up. By nine forty-five they were crouched in the closet of Dr. Bell's home office, waiting to hear the doorbell ring. Ruthie could feel the cold moistness of her palms even though the closet felt airless and warm. Her muscles tightened in odd places, like her throat and her temples. She was sure her thumping heart could be heard throughout the house. *And why is it,* she thought, *that when the last thing you should do is sneeze or cough, that's exactly what you feel like doing?*

"I bet you she'll be here at ten on the dot," Ruthie predicted. She was right. The moment the clock on the computer displayed ten o'clock, the doorbell rang.

They heard Dr. Bell's footsteps across the floor, and

then her voice saying, "Ms. Pommeroy! Thank you so much for coming."

"Please, call me Dora." Dora's buoyant voice sounded through the closet door. "I'm so pleased you asked me. It's not every day that the daughter of Edmund Bell calls for advice."

"Come this way, to the living room. I think this is where I need help the most," Dr. Bell began.

The light from Jack's computer screen glowed in their faces as they watched the two women entering the camera shot. They talked mostly about the furniture in the room, the artwork, the color of the walls. Dora wanted to look at every Edmund Bell photograph and Dr. Bell seemed to enjoy telling her about them. Ruthie couldn't get over how relaxed and poised Dr. Bell appeared—Dora would never suspect that she was setting a trap!

To describe different color schemes, Dora pulled from her tote bag swatches of fabrics and samples of tile and wood. She held them up to the light and compared them to pieces of furniture in the room. Then she pulled a green apple from the bag! Dr. Bell didn't flinch, but Ruthie did. They heard her say something about the color of accent pillows on the sofa. But then the apple went back into her bag. Had they been terribly wrong about Dora? Of course an interior decorator might use apples simply for their color—that was a logical explanation. Ruthie had a sinking feeling in the pit of her stomach.

After ten minutes, Jack nodded to Ruthie, who lifted

her cell phone out of her pocket and dialed. Seconds later, Dr. Bell's office phone rang.

"Forgive me," Dr. Bell said to Dora, "I'm on call this weekend; I'll have to take this." She walked into her office to take the call. Dr. Bell talked into her phone, asking questions about fever and swelling.

Ruthie and Jack listened and silently watched the computer screen. Dora walked around the room, picking up objects, taking notes, and snapping digital pictures. A couple of times she held something in her hands for an extra-long moment, and Ruthie was sure she would put the item in her bag. But she didn't. Then she walked to the other side of the room, coming closer to the camera— really close—reading book titles. Ruthie squelched a gasp and instead whispered into the phone for Dr. Bell to hang up now and go back into the room. Just as she seemed to be about to look directly into the camera, Dr. Bell ended her pretend conversation and reentered the living room. Dora turned to face her, just in time.

"I'm sorry for the interruption," Dr. Bell said.

"No problem. I see we have similar taste in books."

"She didn't take anything!" Ruthie whispered.

"I know. And I'm worried she saw the camera."

The two women talked for a while about some of their favorite books, Dr. Bell having no idea whether or not Dora had pocketed anything. Dora glided around the room as she spoke, moving objects here and there, showing Dr. Bell different possible combinations.

"I'm going to call again," Ruthie whispered as she pushed the redial button. Dr. Bell's office phone rang.

"Excuse me once more," Dr. Bell apologized, and went into her office to take the call.

Ruthie whispered into her phone, "She didn't take anything yet. Stay on the phone longer."

"Yes, of course," Dr. Bell replied, playing along.

"I'll let you know when to hang up," Ruthie said softly.

They listened to Dr. Bell faking a consultation and watched Dora roaming the room again. Her expression looked just as it had when she'd stolen the key from Jack's room: supremely confident. She came to the table next to the sofa, where Ruthie had placed the three objects she thought most likely to tempt her.

Dora picked up the little bronze geometric sculpture, inspected it, and made some notes on her pad. She then picked up the African statue, looked at it with her head tilted slightly, and put it down. Last, she picked up the silver box. She held it in her palm, lifting it to eye level. Then she turned it over, carefully examining the markings.

Ruthie held her breath as Dora walked calmly to her leather bag, slipped the box in, and pulled out a green apple. She put the apple on the table. It looked just like it belonged there. Then she took out a measuring tape and began measuring the room.

Stunned but relieved, Ruthie whispered into the phone, "Okay, Dr. Bell." Dr. Bell pretended to wrap up the conversation and then rejoined Dora in the living room. "I hope it won't be like this all day!" she said. "So what do you think? Can I count on you to work your magic?"

"That's why people call me," Dora said.

As soon as they heard the front door close behind Dora, they spilled out of the closet. Dr. Bell hurried into her office.

"We got her!" Jack whooped, waving the disk that had recorded everything. "I'm just going to burn a couple of copies now."

"What did she steal?" Dr. Bell asked.

"The silver box," Ruthie said. "Just what I had a hunch she'd take."

"Do you think she knew it was from the rooms?" Dr. Bell wanted to know.

"I don't think so," Ruthie answered. "It's been missing from the rooms for such a long time that I don't think it's in the catalogue photos. But she looked at the markings, so she knows it's really old."

Ruthie and Dr. Bell walked into the living room. "And look," Ruthie added, pointing to the table where the box had been. "A green apple."

"Better not touch it," Dr. Bell suggested. "The police might want to dust it for fingerprints."

"Why do you think she does this—leaves green apples?" Ruthie asked.

"In the psychology classes I took in med school, I learned that some criminals are so proud of their cleverness that they want to own the crime. The apple is sort of like her signature, but without giving herself away."

"I'm amazed no one noticed the apples in place of the missing objects," Ruthie said.

"I see how that could happen," Dr. Bell began. "She comes into your home and starts to pick things up and rearrange them, like a con artist's shell game. It confuses you a bit; nothing is in the same place as when she started. And she counts on the fact that most people aren't actually very observant. Then she shows you the apple as part of her color samples, and you assume she has left it inadvertently. But leaving it gives her some perverse satisfaction. Sometimes thieves even have a secret desire to get caught, because deep down they feel guilty."

"But why apples?" Ruthie said.

"That, I can't answer."

Jack, who could hear them from the office, came back into the living room. "The police won't care about her motives when we show them the disk."

"Do you want me to come with you to the police?" Dr. Bell offered.

"We can't do that yet," Ruthie said. "We have to get the key back first."

"And all the stuff she stole from the rooms," Jack added.

"How will you do that?" she asked.

"We're still working on it," Jack admitted.

"But we'll get it all back, don't worry," Ruthie assured her.

ANOTHER PHOTO ALBUM

AT THE GALA THAT EVENING, the museum was filled with people in all sorts of outfits: long ball gowns, tuxedos, artists wearing whatever the spirit moved them to wear. Ruthie and Jack, decked out in vintage clothes from Mrs. McVittie's closet, had different reactions: Ruthie loved the compliments on her retro look, while Jack seemed mostly uncomfortable.

"Let's go up there," Jack said, pointing to the stairway. From the second-floor landing they looked down at the panorama: waiters carrying trays of champagne and hors d'oeuvres, gowns in shimmering fabrics, a small jazz band in the corner enlivening the atmosphere. Ruthie was more interested in the spectacle than Jack, but then she remembered why she was wearing clothes from the 1930s: a young girl's future depended on her action. If Louisa was going to live past that decade, she and Jack had to get busy.

"So this is what people do at a gala?" Jack asked. "Wander around and talk?"

"I guess so."

They watched from the landing for a few more minutes. They heard snippets of conversation from people walking up and down the stairs. Lots of them were talking about the art thefts, saying how glad they were that the thief had been apprehended. For Ruthie and Jack, knowing the truth and being unable to say anything about it magnified the pressure: the man behind bars was innocent and the real thief was still on the loose!

Then Ruthie spotted Dora's unmistakable, nearly colorless blond hair amid the crowd. She was wearing a red dress. "Look—she's down there!"

"Let's go before she sees us," Jack said.

"Should we tell your mom we're going downstairs?" Ruthie wondered.

"Nah. She said earlier that she'd text me if she can't find me when she's ready to leave." They hurried down the stairs and left the main hall, heading into the old wing of the building. It was fun to be in the museum after hours. Most of the museum was open for the event, with only a few galleries off-limits, but almost everyone stayed in the main hall for the gala.

Without the sound of people talking in the galleries they passed through, it was somewhat eerie. Ruthie almost expected the paintings and sculptures to come alive and speak to them. Downstairs, Gallery 11 was empty.

"This is great!" Jack said. "It will make things so much easier."

"You ready?" Ruthie asked.

"Ready." Jack reached into his pocket and handed the metal square to Ruthie. In seconds they were slipping under the door. Inside, Ruthie dropped the square, they grew back to full size in the corridor and Jack picked up the square—the whole process like the steps of a dance they could do without a thought. The two of them raced down the corridor to E27, the French library that led them to Paris and, with luck, to Louisa. Jack took the climbing ladder from his other pocket and secured it to the ledge. They shrank again for the long climb.

"I really hope her family is there today," Ruthie said, stepping off the last rung of the ladder and onto the ledge.

"We'll find her this time," Jack promised.

Without so much as a glance through the viewing window to watch out for people, they entered the beautiful room. And even though they were in a hurry to find Louisa, they couldn't resist lingering a bit in the room, knowing there was no one who could see them through the glass.

Jack picked up a red leather book with gold decoration from the circular coffee table and opened it. "Hey, look at this!"

"What is it?"

He held it open for her to see: an album filled with black-and-white photos of people in a city that did not look like the Paris of today. The clothing styles were of the period of the room and maybe earlier. It looked like a typical collection of family photos. Then Ruthie came across a photo with a face she recognized.

"Louisa!"

They turned the pages and saw more photos of Louisa and her family.

"I bet this album is what is making this room alive," Ruthie said. "See what the last pictures are of." Ruthie remembered Sophie's journal and the empty pages at the end, pages that had magically been filled in after they had changed the course of Sophie's life.

The last photos showed the family in Paris; the final one was of the Meyer family standing in front of 7, rue Le Tasse. Louisa looked no older than the day they had met her. All the pages after that were blank.

"That's the last picture . . . we've got to find her!" Ruthie exclaimed.

Jack placed the album down exactly as he had found it and they headed out to the balcony. Ruthie led the way down the spiral staircase.

The courtyard garden was unchanged, with the fragrant roses still in full bloom. They lifted the latchkey from the hook on the wall, opened the gate and walked out onto the sidewalks of Paris.

They wasted no time and went directly to rue Le Tasse, but when they neared the corner Ruthie stopped and pointed to the street sign.

"Look," she said. "Rue Benjamin Franklin. Remember how Sophie said they all thought he was so interesting?"

"So they named a street after him. That's kinda cool," Jack said.

They turned onto rue Le Tasse and walked the short distance to number 7, at the end of the block. Ruthie took a deep breath and pushed the buzzer.

Ten seconds passed, seeming like minutes. The woman at the window who had spoken to them so curtly a few days earlier peered from behind the lace curtain and then walked away from the window into the darkness of her apartment. She gave them shivers. Then they heard a voice calling from overhead. They looked up to see Louisa on the balcony waving.

"*Bonjour,* Ruthie and Jack! Please come up to the fourth floor!" They heard the click of the big door unlocking. The mean woman returned to the window and leaned out, yelling something up to Louisa. Ruthie couldn't understand what she was saying, but they could hear its icy intent. They slipped inside before the woman could turn her attention to them.

They found themselves in a covered walkway wide enough for cars. Directly in front of them a courtyard opened to the sky, a few 1930s automobiles parked around the center. On their right was a door to what must have been the apartment of the grumpy window lady, and on the left, three steps led to an entry hall. The floor was

marble and a spiral staircase wrapped around an elevator that resembled a fancy birdcage.

"Stairs or elevator?" Ruthie asked, reluctant to climb into the contraption.

"Elevator, for sure," Jack said. "It's awesome."

They slid open the accordion-style metal gate. The elevator was only big enough for two, maybe three people at most. A brass panel with black buttons marked the floors. "Fourth floor, right?" Jack asked, pushing the button.

"Right." Ruthie's nerves jangled as they ascended, and she wasn't sure if this antique appliance or their imminent meeting was the cause. She tried to keep her mind focused on what she was going to say to Louisa. This couldn't be a simple friendly visit. They slowly passed the first three floors and then the elevator stopped abruptly, giving a little bounce, at the fourth. Jack slid open the gate.

There was only one door in the small hallway and no doorbell, but in the center of the door was a knob that looked like it should be turned, so Ruthie did. The highly polished metal felt cool to her touch. Through the heavy wooden door she heard the clang of a real bell.

Louisa opened the door and hugged them like old friends. "Hello! I am so happy to see you; I worried that I might not! Please come in. *Mutter, Vater, komm hier!*" Ruthie and Jack knew she was speaking German, but it sounded just like "Mother, Father, come here."

The apartment in front of them was quite elegant and

large. It looked exactly like something out of the Thorne Rooms.

"Wow, nice place," Jack said.

"Thank you." Louisa led them into the living room. The off-white walls looked like they'd been decorated with cake icing: carved flowers and ribbons ran along the tops near the equally ornate ceiling. An old smoky mirror hung over the marble fireplace, and floor-to-ceiling velvet curtains framed the French doors that led to small balconies overlooking rue Le Tasse and the Jardins du Trocadéro. The furniture was just as lavish.

"Welcome," Louisa's mother greeted them as she entered. Her German accent was thicker than Louisa's. "You must be the Americans Louisa told us about. Please sit down." She motioned to a silk-covered sofa.

"May I offer you some tea?"

"No, thank you," Ruthie replied.

"What have you been doing during your visit to Paris?" Louisa asked. "You should have come to see me sooner!"

"We did come," Ruthie said. "The woman downstairs in the window told us you were away in the country and wouldn't be back until yesterday."

Louisa and her mother looked at each other, saying something in German. Louisa explained, "We were here, but perhaps just out for an hour or two. She doesn't like us and gives us trouble."

"What kind of trouble?" Jack asked.

"She is our *concierge*—how do you say it in English? Doorman? Sometimes she won't give us our mail for days, and she tells visitors we have moved away!"

"Enough of such unpleasantness," Mrs. Meyer broke in. "How do you like Paris?"

"We like it very much, thank you," Ruthie answered. "It's a beautiful city."

"Louisa tells me you are from Chicago."

"That's right."

"We have never been to Chicago. Only New York. Someday I should like to see all of the United States."

"We should, Mutter," Louisa enjoined. "We could visit them in Chicago!"

"Perhaps when all these unsettling events are concluded, we shall." The way Mrs. Meyer said "unsettling events" made Ruthie think she didn't understand how bad it was going to be. At that moment Louisa's father came in.

"Good afternoon! You must be Jack and Ruthie from Chicago!" He strode over to shake hands. "Will you stay for lunch?" Only a hint of German could be heard in his English.

"You must stay!" Louisa insisted.

Thinking fast, Jack said, "We have to meet our dad in a little less than an hour."

"Well, then, that will give you just enough time." Dr. Meyer was the kind of person you couldn't say no to.

They sat at a long, formally set table in the dining room. Dr. Meyer was seated at the head and Mrs. Meyer at the other end. A maid appeared and went from place to place, serving soup. Ruthie wasn't sure which forks and spoons to use, and neither was Jack. He looked at her and made a funny face, which almost made her laugh. Ruthie glanced at Louisa, who was holding the rounder spoon, so she picked hers up as well. As soon as Mrs. Meyer took a taste, Louisa began. Ruthie followed suit. It was some kind of potato soup, and it was delicious.

"So, what does your father do that brings him to Paris?" Dr. Meyer asked.

"Import-export," Jack said.

"Wine?" Dr. Meyer asked.

"Exactly," Jack said.

"Tell me, what does he think of the current world situation?" he inquired.

"He has a lot of opinions about that," Ruthie said, relieved he had brought up the subject.

"I am most interested. Could you explain?"

"He knows lots of people in business and government. They predict there will be a war with Hitler," Ruthie answered.

Louisa's mother put down her spoon.

"Our father is trying to finish up his business in France because he thinks it will be very bad here too," Jack added.

"This is what some have been saying," Dr. Meyer said. Louisa's eyes were wide.

"And what is President Roosevelt's view?" Mrs. Meyer asked. Her expression had gotten very serious.

"I'm not positive about the president's position," Jack admitted. "But I am sure that all of our dad's Jewish friends think their relatives should come to the United States—as soon as they can."

"He says it won't be safe, even here in Paris. You must believe us," Ruthie implored, hoping that her voice carried the urgency she felt.

"But surely Hitler can't control Paris," Mrs. Meyer said in disbelief.

"Dad and his business partners are sure he will," Jack responded.

"Did anybody think Hitler could do the things he's already done in Germany?" Ruthie asked.

Dr. Meyer nodded when Ruthie said that, and then he was very quiet; Mrs. Meyer looked at him for a response. "We could stay with our family in New York," he said after a moment.

"You should. You really should," Ruthie pressed, finding it difficult to stay calm.

"But what about our home in Berlin?" Louisa sounded quite upset.

"Home is wherever we are together." Dr. Meyer reached over to her and gave her hand a squeeze. "Besides, it looks as though the German government won't be giving me back my license to practice medicine anytime soon. I received another denial yesterday. I want to work."

Just then the front door opened and a disheveled-looking boy tumbled in. He appeared about a year or two older than Louisa and was wearing some sort of team uniform. His curly dark hair was messed up and he had dirt—and a very angry look—on his face.

Mrs. Meyer rushed to him. "Jacob! What happened?"

"After the game some of the other team's players followed me home. They started fighting with me," he said, taking off his sport shoes.

"Are you all right? Did they hurt you?" Mrs. Meyer fussed over him.

"I'm fine. They called me names. So I fought back and they finally stopped."

Dr. Meyer got up from the table to see his son. Louisa leaned forward and said softly to them, "That's my brother, Jacob. There are boys on the teams who fight with anyone who is Jewish. It's happened before."

"That stinks," Jack said.

After Jacob went to clean up, his parents whispered to each other in the entryway for some time before coming back to the dining room.

A few minutes later Jacob—now all cleaned up—came to the table, where the maid had just set a bowl of soup for him. "I'm hungry!"

"Jacob! Your manners!" Mrs. Meyer admonished. "This is Ruthie and Jack, Louisa's friends who are visiting from Chicago. This is my son, Jacob."

"Pleased to meet you," Jacob came around to shake hands with them. Jack surprised Ruthie by actually standing up to greet him.

"What's your sport?" Jack asked.

"Football," Jacob replied. "Do you play?"

"Yeah, some. We call it soccer in the States. I play on our school team."

"How about baseball; do you ever play that?" Jacob asked eagerly.

"Yeah. It's a summer sport, though."

"Ruthie, Jack, you two have been most helpful," Dr. Meyer said. "I had been thinking about the possibility of an extended visit to our relatives in New York. What you've said has brought me to a decision."

"I think it's a really good idea," Ruthie said emphatically.

"And your father is so certain that this war will take place?" Mrs. Meyer asked.

"It's gonna happen, for sure," Jack said.

"You can't stay in Europe with the war coming," Ruthie stressed. "Your whole family would be in danger."

Dr. Meyer declared, "We will go."

Jacob smiled at the prospect. "I could join a baseball team! Let's stay long enough for me to play for at least one whole season." He turned to Jack to explain, "No one plays baseball here in Europe. We could see the Yankees play!"

Frieda, the little dachshund, appeared at Louisa's side. Louisa picked up the dog, burying her face in the shiny coat.

"Louisa, *liebchen*," her mother began.

"I can't help it. I miss home. I want to go home." Tears streamed down her cheeks.

Even knowing without a doubt that what she and Jack had done was the right thing, Ruthie still felt partially responsible for this terrible upheaval in Louisa's world.

"I'm sorry, Louisa. But you'll get to go back to Berlin someday." Ruthie hoped that was the right thing to say. Louisa sniffled and smiled.

"Thanks." She wiped her tears with her napkin. "Can we bring Frieda, Vater?"

"Of course; she is a member of the family!" he answered.

Jack caught Ruthie's eye and tapped his watch. Jacob noticed. "That's an interesting watch. I've never seen one like that!"

Jack wore a chunky black watch with extra dials on the face and set pins on the side. "They're pretty common in Chicago," he responded.

"I'm afraid we're going to have to leave," Ruthie apologized. "Our father will be worried if we're late."

"Are you sure?" Louisa asked. "At least give me your address in Chicago." Louisa jumped up and retrieved some paper and a pencil from a nearby desk.

Before Ruthie could make any excuses the paper was on the table in front of her, the whole family watching. Ruthie started writing, knowing full well that any letter Louisa sent to her would never reach her; the building she lived in hadn't even been built until the 1960s. Then she remembered Mrs. McVittie's building; it was old and had been built early in the twentieth century. She wrote "in care of" and then Mrs. McVittie's name and address.

They said goodbye and wished each other good luck, and Louisa hugged Ruthie. The whole family stepped into the hall with them as they waited for the elevator. It arrived and the two visitors got in. Jack slid the gate closed in the elevator, and they descended out of Louisa's life.

· · · 13 · · ·
THE CURSE

"**I** HEAR SOMETHING," JACK CAUTIONED. "LISTEN."

They were standing in room E27, having just finished climbing up the spiral staircase. They'd been away from the gala for nearly an hour.

Ruthie listened for a moment. "I don't hear anything. What was it?"

"Not sure. It might have been the corridor door opening and closing." He walked through the room and back out to the ledge. Ruthie followed, stopping as Jack looked carefully before going all the way out to the enormous space. "C'mon," he said, judging it to be all clear.

Then Ruthie heard something too. From farther along in the corridor came the sound of what she thought must be the stepladder—the one Dora had asked the workmen to leave for her—unfolding. They hurried to the next corner and peeked. Ruthie put her hand to her mouth.

At the midpoint of the corridor, they saw her, about five feet away from them. Dora, in her red cocktail dress and high heels, had just climbed to the top of the stepladder—which put her feet level with the ledge. Ruthie knew instantly what she was about to do. They stood watching; she opened her small evening bag and reached into it. In a flash, they saw happen to Dora what they had only ever seen happen to each other. Her hair was pulled back tightly but they still could see the effect of the breeze as it ruffled the hem of her silky dress. They watched as her eyes widened, and in a blur Ruthie saw the red dress hang too loosely for a second, then shrink to fit her, over and over again. It was amazing to see how swiftly and fluidly the magic acted on her. From as far away as Ruthie and Jack were, they could still see Dora's astonished reaction.

In a moment, Dora was just under six inches tall. She inhaled deeply, smoothed her hair and stepped off the top of the ladder and onto the ledge, disappearing from their view as she entered the framework of Room E23.

Jack looked at Ruthie. "What's in that room—do you know?"

"I think it's a French dining room. What do you think we should do now?"

"Keep an eye on her."

"What if she sees us?" Ruthie asked.

"She already knows we know about the magic. She owes us the explanation, so we'll just ask for one. And the key."

Sometimes Jack's clarity astonished Ruthie. *Of course that's what we should do,* she thought.

Ruthie guessed Dora wouldn't be in the room too long. "I don't think it's one of her favorites. Let's see what she does next."

Sure enough, in about a minute, she came out again, and walked along the corridor. The next room was E24. "That's Sophie's room!" Ruthie whispered. "We can't let her take anything from in there."

"Then let's go and stop her before she does."

Ruthie knew he was right—they had to confront her. They hurried to the entrance of the room. Jack looked at Ruthie and stepped aside for her to go in first.

Dora's back was to them. She stood in front of the fireplace, inspecting objects on the mantel; a mirror over it reflected Ruthie's image as she entered the room. It also reflected Dora's face, so Ruthie could see her look of shock and then a quick correction to surprise.

"Ruthie! And Jack!" Turning to face them, she spoke as if they'd bumped into each other on the street. "What are you doing here?"

"We came with Jack's mom to the gala and wanted to come down here while we had the chance," Ruthie answered.

"You must be wondering how I did this," she said. "And I could ask you the same thing, couldn't I?"

Jack answered fast. "We know lots of ways to shrink."

"Really?" Dora arched an eyebrow.

"You have our key, don't you?" Ruthie asked, trying to remain calm.

"Well, yes, I have the key. I borrowed it from you two, just as you two borrowed it from whomever you borrowed it from."

"Why didn't you just ask?" Ruthie said.

"You see, I had a bit of a problem," Dora began. "The curator gave me permission to remove a few items from the rooms to study them for my thesis. This was about two months ago. Most of the items were miniatures and stayed small. But a few of the items suddenly grew large as I was leaving the museum. Naturally, I was shocked and had no idea how that could happen!"

"And you didn't know how to put the full-sized objects back," Jack finished for her.

"That's exactly right," Dora said, warming to her story. "I could put the miniature pieces back in their places, but I didn't know what to do with the ones that grew."

"I can see what a big problem that was, can't you, Jack?" Ruthie said.

"Really big," he agreed.

"And that day when I took you back into the corridor and you told me about the magic, I could barely believe it. But at the same time it made sense because I'd experienced those objects growing right in my tote bag." She watched their expressions carefully to see if Ruthie and Jack believed her.

"But why didn't you tell me all this before?"

"I didn't want to get you mixed up in my mess. And I only needed to use the key to put the objects back."

"Have you put them back?" Ruthie asked.

"Not yet. I was too nervous to try the key while the museum was open. I thought tonight would be the perfect time to at least find out if the key would work for me. But it would have been tricky to bring the objects back during the gala." She held up the small evening bag she carried to emphasize the point. "But tell me, how did you get small without the key?"

"My phone!" Jack said, reaching into his pocket, pretending it was vibrating. He looked at the blank screen as though reading a text. "It's my mom—she's looking for us. We'd better get out of here now!"

Ruthie had an idea. "If you come back tomorrow with all the objects, we'll help you put them back—and show you more of the magic."

"But the museum will be open," Dora said.

"No problem," Ruthie insisted. "We'll show you everything."

"What do you mean, everything?" Dora asked.

"There are a lot more secrets to the magic," Jack continued.

"I'm not sure I can bring everything back tomorrow . . ." Dora was stalling, but Ruthie could tell she was intrigued.

"Some of the painted dioramas are alive," Ruthie added to sweeten the enticement.

"Alive?" Dora asked.

"Yes. Like time portals," Ruthie explained. "We've gone back to the eighteenth and nineteenth centuries. We've met people from then."

"Have you ever . . . brought anything back from the past?"

They had no intention of telling her that was impossible, that things from the past disappear when they end up in the rooms. "We never thought of that," Ruthie replied.

"But you mean, I—you—could meet Rembrandt? Or Picasso before he was famous?" She wasn't really speaking to them when she said this. It was more like she was thinking aloud. "You could buy a painting for almost nothing!"

Ruthie observed a steely flicker of greed in Dora's eyes, and at that moment she no longer looked beautiful to her.

"We'll even show you the curse," Jack put in, pitching a new twist.

"Curse?" Dora looked at Jack like he'd just interrupted the most delicious thought she'd ever had. "What curse?"

"Duchess Christina's curse, placed on people who disrespect the magic," he improvised. "We don't know if it's true."

"But we didn't think anything like this was possible before we experienced it—so the curse could be true," Ruthie tossed in as embellishment.

"C'mon." Jack hurried them along. "We have to go."

They left the room, making sure they were behind Dora so she couldn't steal anything on her way out. While Dora was turning toward the stepladder, Ruthie grabbed Jack's hand, tossed the metal square over the ledge and jumped.

Dora turned just in time to see them growing in midair.

The whole thing happened so swiftly—including Jack picking up the square and putting it in his pocket—that she didn't get even a glimpse of it.

"How did you do that?" she exclaimed, her mouth agape.

"Nothing to it," the full-sized Jack said to the tiny woman on the ledge. "You just toss the key to the floor. Try it."

"I don't know . . . ," she began.

"Really, Dora, don't be afraid," Ruthie coaxed. Being so large in comparison made Ruthie feel very powerful.

"All right. Here goes." She threw the key to the floor and took a timid step forward, growing in midair.

Jack scooped up the key before its odd tinkling had even stopped and put it in his other pocket. It couldn't have been easier.

Dora landed awkwardly in her high heels. "Whew. I don't know if I like that!"

"It gets easier," Ruthie assured her.

Dora looked on the floor around her. "Where's the key?"

Jack, who had already started down the corridor, turned and flashed a smile at her. "You'd just shrink again if you pick it up in here. The magic doesn't work on guys."

Dora looked as if she suspected she'd been outfoxed, but there was nothing she could do about it without admitting her real motives. She squared her shoulders and followed.

When they arrived at the exit, Jack asked, "You have a

· 192 ·

key to the door, right, Dora?" Ruthie knew he had no intention of taking either Duchess Christina's key or the square out of his pocket.

"Yes, but how did you get in?" she asked.

"We'll explain it all tomorrow morning. Meet us here at eleven," Ruthie instructed.

"Yes. I'll be here."

"Don't forget," Ruthie reminded her, "bring all the objects you need to put back. We'll help you!"

Dora smiled less easily than usual at Ruthie, smoothed her hair one more time, and turned the key in the lock. The three of them walked into the empty Gallery 11, the door locking behind them.

Ruthie spent the night at Jack's. She made a quick call to Mrs. McVittie and had her nightly check-in with her parents before putting on her pajamas. Jack lay in his bed up in his sleeping loft while Ruthie bunked on the couch in his living room.

"Can you believe it?" Jack said from above. "It was so easy."

"I know. But you know what I can't believe?"

"What?"

"I can't believe she stole the *Mayflower*. Of all the stuff she could've taken. Somebody's bound to notice soon, besides us."

"Yeah. Incredible," Jack responded through a yawn.

"Do you think we really saved Louisa and her family?"

"Her dad seemed like a smart guy. Don't forget, they'd already figured out that they should leave Germany. He said they would go to New York," Jack answered.

Ruthie yawned. "I hope Dora shows up tomorrow."

"You saw how interested she was in getting her hands on old art. She'll be there."

"I hope—" Ruthie started to speak, but was interrupted by another yawn. "I hope she brings everything."

The last thing Ruthie heard was Jack saying, "We'll find out tomorrow," and then she was asleep.

In Ruthie's dream she was back in her own bed, with Claire snoring softly on the other side of the room, as usual. For some reason, Ruthie got up and walked into the hall past the bathroom and her parents' room until she stood in front of another room, one that she had never seen in their apartment before. *That's funny, I've lived here all my life; how come I never knew we had this room?* She took a step to enter it, but hit a hard surface—the wall. Then she realized that the room was really a trompe l'oeil painting. As she stood marveling at how convincing it was, someone appeared in it. A tall woman with ghostly white hair walked around looking for something. "Dora?" Ruthie called out, but the woman's face was in shadow and she couldn't be certain it was her. Then Ruthie noticed that the room was filled with boxes of all sorts, many just like some in the Thorne Rooms. There was the silver box that Caroline Bell had taken, and one that Ruthie recognized from Sophie's room. And there was

Jack's bento box. The woman examined the boxes, opening all of them and putting something in. "Dora, is that you?" Ruthie called to her again, but the woman didn't respond. Ruthie watched her looking in each box and then could see that the woman was actually placing apples in them. "Dora!" Ruthie nearly shouted. But the painting began to fade slowly, and Ruthie found herself staring at a plain white wall. She walked back to her bedroom, climbed into her bed and closed her eyes, listening to her sister's steady purr.

· · · 14 · · ·

BEHIND THE CURTAINS

IN THE MORNING RUTHIE AND Jack stopped at Mrs. McVittie's before their eleven o'clock meeting with Dora. She fed them breakfast while they told her everything. Then Jack called Caroline Bell to finalize the last steps in the plan.

"All set," he said, closing his cell phone. "She's ready."

"With all this excitement I almost forgot to show you this," Mrs. McVittie announced, getting up from the table and going into the dining room. She retrieved a leather-bound scrapbook and magnifying glass from her book-covered table. She set them down in the kitchen and opened the book to the most recent entries, the clippings from last weekend's newspaper. They saw the photo of Ruthie and Jack standing with Mr. Bell, a large crowd behind them.

"I was putting these in my album last night and

something caught my eye." She handed them her magnifying glass.

They looked through the glass and cried out at the same time: "Dora!"

"That's right! She was there. I knew when I met her in the museum the next morning that I'd seen her somewhere before."

"Why wouldn't she tell us she'd been there?" Ruthie asked.

"She never actually denied it, did she?" Mrs. McVittie pointed out.

"But she acted like she had no idea who we were, when really she did," Ruthie said.

"Do you think she planned on meeting us?" Jack wondered.

"I wouldn't doubt it," Mrs. McVittie answered. "Dora Pommeroy doesn't strike me as the kind of person who lets anything happen by chance."

As Mrs. McVittie spoke, Ruthie had that funny sensation that comes when a dream you've had is trying to wriggle back into your consciousness. First she remembered the hallway in her apartment and the trompe l'oeil room appearing, and then the whole dream flooded back. "Jack—we still haven't found out who wrote on the note in your bento box," Ruthie said.

"Wow—I sort of forgot about it with everything else happening," Jack said.

"I had a dream last night that made me think it was Dora," Ruthie said, remembering the shadowy figure slipping apples into boxes.

Mrs. McVittie spoke up. "If she is the author, it would explain why she went to Edmund Bell's opening; she had already found the note in the bento box, and then when she heard your names associated with Edmund, she wanted to see you."

"She must've been the one who wrote on the note," Jack said.

"Let's try to ask her today," Ruthie suggested. "She trusts us, I think."

"Look at the time, you two. You don't want to be late." Mrs. McVittie started to clear the breakfast dishes. "And don't forget, Ruthie, your parents will be back by suppertime."

Her parents! Ruthie had almost forgotten they were coming home today. She was looking forward to seeing them, but there was a lot to get done in a little time!

Jack and Ruthie rushed out into the beautiful Chicago Sunday, the kind of day they ordinarily would have spent outside. Sunlight reflected in the windows of the skyscrapers, and the city sparkled. They ran nearly all the way from Mrs. McVittie's apartment, arriving at the museum ten minutes before eleven. The two of them sat on the steps by one of the bronze lions to wait for Dora.

After a bit Ruthie checked her watch: 11:01. "What time does your watch say?" she asked Jack.

"A minute after eleven," he answered.

"She's never late. Something's wrong," Ruthie said.

"Could be our watches are a little fast."

"True," Ruthie admitted, although she could feel the hollow of her stomach deepening.

People walked by in a steady stream. No Dora.

At seven minutes past eleven Ruthie worried aloud, "You know, Jack, she doesn't have to show up or bring back any of the objects. They're really valuable antiques that she could sell for a lot of money. And she knows we're not going to tell anyone about the shrinking and the magic."

"That's possible," Jack conceded. "But I still think her curiosity will make her show up."

"I hope you're right." Just then Ruthie felt a hand on her shoulder. She nearly jumped out of her skin.

"Ruthie, Jack," the cool voice said from behind. "Here you are; I've been waiting inside for you."

Calming herself, and hoping Dora hadn't overheard them, Ruthie responded, "Hi, Dora."

Jack stood up too. "I guess we never told you where to meet us. Did you bring everything?" Jack glanced at the large leather tote bag that she always carried. It looked pretty full. She also held a shopping bag from which he could see the tip of a ship's mast poking out from some bubble wrap. "That's the *Mayflower* model from A1, isn't it?"

"Very good, Jack. You do know the rooms well, don't you?"

"Not really, not like Ruthie. It's just that the model is one of my favorite things."

"It is a really special piece. It has a name written on the bottom," Dora said.

"We know: Thomas Wilcox. We met him," Jack said.

"You met him?" Dora was astounded. "Was he in the room?"

"No. We went out into his time, into the seventeenth century," Jack explained casually.

"That's amazing!" Her eyes narrowed a bit.

Ruthie was certain that Dora was thinking about all the treasures she was hoping to lay claim to from beyond the rooms. "C'mon, let's go." Ruthie led them up the steps.

With Dora's museum ID tag around her neck, they had no problem bringing the shopping bag into the museum, and the three of them made a beeline for the stairs. Since it was such a nice day outside, Gallery 11 was relatively empty. Dora smiled brightly at the guard on duty. "Hello, Louis. I've got some work to do in the corridor, and these are my interns." She spoke with complete confidence.

"Aren't you the two who found Edmund Bell's photographs?"

"Yep, that's us," Jack answered.

"I thought I'd been seeing you around here lately," the guard commented. "Any friend of Edmund's is a friend of mine. You three go right ahead. Let me know if you need anything."

"Thank you," Dora said. She led the way past the information booth to the American rooms' access door, the one Ruthie and Jack had not been able to squeeze under. Dora used her key to let them in. It was all so easy.

"So how do we do this?" Dora asked.

"First," Ruthie said, "why don't you show us all the objects that we need to put back?"

"Right," Jack agreed. "Let's get that done, and then we can show you how the magic gets you into the past worlds."

"And the curse? I'm very interested in learning more about that," Dora asked.

"For sure. We'll tell you all about that!" Ruthie enthused. "How many American pieces do you have?"

"Let's see." She hesitated. "There's the *Mayflower* in here." Dora raised the shopping bag. Then she reached into her big leather bag, pulling out an unusual-looking object. "This is from one of the rooms from the South."

"Is that one of the picture-viewing things—a stereopti-something?" Jack asked, intrigued by the wood and metal instrument.

"A stereopticon," Dora answered. "Good antiques like this are hard to find."

"I know where that belongs," Ruthie said. "In the Georgia room, right next to the Charleston room."

"What else?" Jack continued.

"Just this." Dora pulled a small silver goblet from her big bag.

"Hmmm." Ruthie tilted her head. "What room is that from?"

"It came from a Maryland dining room." Dora's eyes caught a glint from the shiny sterling piece as she held it close to her face. "It's exquisite."

"Is that everything?" Ruthie prodded.

"Of course," Dora responded. Ruthie wasn't sure if she believed her—why should she? Ruthie thought it very likely that Dora was scheming to put everything back now and steal it again later. But Dora did seem motivated to follow their directions—for the moment, at least—so they would reward her with information.

"Let's have the *Mayflower*. That should go back first." Jack reached for the shopping bag.

Dora nervously clutched it. "Are you sure? Couldn't we do some exploring first?"

"I think it would be smart to get everything put away before we do that. What if someone comes back here for some reason and starts asking questions? You could get in big trouble, Dora," Ruthie replied.

"Oh—oh, I see. Yes, of course." She grudgingly surrendered the bag.

"Let's have the goblet and the stereopticon too." Ruthie put her hand out for them.

"But I would love to put something back myself," Dora complained.

"First things first." Jack sounded terribly bossy. Dora obeyed and handed over the two antiques. They put everything in the shopping bag for the shrinking process, being especially careful with Thomas' ship. "Ready?" Jack asked.

"Yep," Ruthie answered.

Jack reached into a pocket for the key and dropped it into her open palm. Ruthie had gotten used to the magic of the metal square and noticed the difference right away, as if the key's magic was more powerful, the process smoother and faster. Like the difference between riding in a really new car and an old one. In an instant, Ruthie and the three objects were mouse-sized.

For a horrible moment, Ruthie recognized the disadvantage she was at—Dora was now an evil giant before her. She was glad Jack remained big.

Jack gently picked up tiny Ruthie and the shopping bag, setting them down gingerly on the ledge near A1, the room from the time of the Salem witch trials—Thomas' room. "Don't forget to look before you go in."

Ruthie took the *Mayflower* and stepped through the framework and into the small room that led to the main one. She tiptoed to the doorway and peeked in. The beautiful wooden surfaces glowed and the huge fireplace felt so inviting. The mug in which she had found Caroline Bell's pink barrette hung on the hook right where Ruthie had put it. The lack of museum visitors made it easy—she could go right in.

Everything was unchanged since their last visit, except

it was too quiet—it was as if the sound had been turned off on a TV and there was just the picture. But something happened as she walked across the wide wood floorboards and lifted the *Mayflower* to its home on the mantel. First she heard the tinkling, bell-like sound that she'd heard when she touched Christina's book. It was both everywhere and far away and lasted only a few seconds before subsiding. Then she heard life—not sounds from the museum, but the normal sounds of outdoors that one notices only if they aren't there. She heard the wind in the trees, birds singing, children playing. She hurried behind the tall bench and through the door to the room's entryway and looked outside—yes, it was alive, all right! She was tempted to rush out and find Thomas again, but she knew Jack would need her in the corridor.

"Mission number one accomplished!" Ruthie said as she arrived back out at the ledge. "What's next?"

"The Maryland dining room," Jack replied.

It didn't take Ruthie too long to scramble along the narrow walkway. Jack and Dora followed.

"Dora, do you remember where the goblet goes?" Ruthie asked.

"Yes; put it on the small side table, the one with the mirror over it." Dora looked pained.

"Got it." Ruthie stepped into the framework and into a side room. From there she could see the entire space: a late eighteenth-century room with walls painted the color of a robin's egg and a crystal chandelier that captured and refracted the light coming from the windows. She saw a portrait of a woman in an oval frame, dressed like Betsy Ross or Abigail Adams, she thought. Maybe this was the woman's room. Ruthie liked her face and wished she had more time to look at all the other objects.

Ruthie pulled back as two people walked into view. She waited until their voices subsided, then stepped in. She placed the goblet where it belonged and listened as the sparkling sound of the magic resonated around her for just a few seconds. She looked out the window at the view of a beautiful formal garden in summer. There were no people in the garden, but she saw two squirrels chasing each other, their fluffy tails bobbing about as they jumped from branch to branch in the gently swaying trees.

She left the room and returned to Jack and Dora in the corridor. "Okay—last stop, A30, the Georgia room."

"But I thought we'd get to look in the rooms," Dora complained again.

"Don't worry; we will. It's just that the really great stuff is on the European side," Jack answered. The look of frustration on her face did not subside.

At this point, Ruthie needed to be on the other side of the corridor, so Jack lifted her off the ledge and carried her over. She sat cross-legged in the deep creases of his giant palm and rather enjoyed the ride.

He set her down, now with only the stereopticon to return. She remembered that it belonged on the table toward the back of the room—no need to ask Dora. She made her way to the entrance. A30 was a double parlor, meaning it was really two rooms, one in front of the other. She found herself in the rear of the two, which were decorated in the same style, with the same lush red velvets and opulent gold satins. Ruthie had looked at this room many times in the catalogue, but it seemed far more elaborate when she was actually inside of it. How many servants—slaves—were needed to support this lifestyle? she wondered.

Ruthie looked through the front room toward the viewing window as she crept farther in. All clear. Interestingly, the room felt alive already, and she listened carefully for more telltale sounds. Yes, she heard life beyond the heavily curtained bay windows, muffled and distant but nevertheless real. She placed the stereopticon on the table where it belonged, next to a small stack of books. As she predicted, the wind-chime-like sound did not start up. Clearly, this stereopticon, though old, was not the animating object of room A30. Ruthie took one more long look around the grand space, speculating about what the magic item might be.

"Okay, we've got all the American stuff put back," Ruthie said as she reappeared, already having decided that she was going one room back, to A29, Phoebe's room. She started in that direction.

"Where are you going?" Dora asked impatiently.

"I have to check something in the next room. Jack, do you have the you-know-what?"

He patted a pocket that held the square.

"Is it doing anything?" Ruthie asked.

Jack opened his pocket just enough to get a glimpse. "Yep, glowing. But just a little."

"What? What are you two talking about?" This was all more than Dora could tolerate. "You said you'd teach me all about the magic."

"When we get to the European corridor we'll explain," Jack replied.

As Jack spoke, Ruthie slipped into the framework of A29. The museum was still empty enough for her to walk right into the room through the door she had left ajar last time. The tall cabinet stood near the front; Ruthie went straight over to it, as though an invisible magnet pulled her. Standing directly in front of it, she saw the curtains hanging behind glass panels but realized she couldn't easily open the doors; there were no knobs to pull, only two keyholes. But there was a drawer below with two knobs. She pulled the knobs, and the drawer slid open, revealing a single key on a gold cord. Ruthie slid it into the keyhole; it fit. She gave it a half turn and heard the sound of the latch moving.

The hinges creaked and resisted when she pulled the door, but it opened. Inside, she spied a single object: a leather-bound book, held closed not by a locking clasp but by two leather ties. It had no gold decorations, no markings of any kind; it was well used and obviously very old. She picked it up, closed the cabinet and walked through the French doors to the covered porch. Here, she would be invisible to anyone from the nineteenth century who might happen by, and out of sight to museum visitors as well. Birds flew about in the nearby oaks, and the scent of garden flowers was sweet and strong. She sat down on the painted white floorboards, warm from the sun. How lovely it would be to sit and enjoy the moment and have all the time she wanted to explore this book, this world. But Jack couldn't hold off Dora indefinitely.

She opened the book to somewhere in the middle. At first she couldn't read it—it was all handwritten, and some things seemed misspelled. Ink smudges dappled the margins. It appeared to be a ledger of some kind. Ruthie thumbed through a few pages. She saw lists in columns with quantities, sometimes broken up with short para- graphs. Once she became accustomed to the writing she could read most of it and realized that these were recipes of a sort, or formulas.

Ruthie went back to the first page to see if there was a title. In larger and careful handwriting, she read:

Secret and complete record of elixirs, balms, extracts, curatives, and potions, penned to perfection by Phoebe Monroe, of the Gillis family, of Charleston, commenced in AD 1840.

Phoebe!

She gently turned to the back to see if all the pages were filled in. The book was complete, but—to Ruthie's amazement—tucked in after the last page was the spiral notebook she had given Phoebe! There, on the cover, was what Ruthie had written: *A gift to Phoebe, from Ruthie Stewart.* She opened it. The handwriting was in pencil, less skillful yet carefully lettered along the blue lines of the paper. She could barely take her eyes off the paper, yellowed and brittle with age. It was tangible evidence that she and Jack had actually gone back in time and that this notebook had been written in more than a hundred and fifty years ago!

She wanted to run out to show Jack, but she didn't want to let Dora see it or even know of its existence. No, it would be wiser to put it safely back in the cabinet. She would come back to it another time.

···15···

A WHISKERED MONSTER

WHILE RUTHIE WAS IN ROOM A29, Jack "explained" things to Dora. By the time Ruthie returned to the ledge, he had embellished the powers of the magic so much that the magic as it existed seemed dull in comparison. He described how some European rooms enabled them to speak in a foreign language, and that in one room he had actually levitated!

"So the curse says that if anyone uses the magic for personal gain or that if the objects are separated from the rooms for too long, something horrible will happen to that person," he finished.

"Where does it say that?" she demanded.

"In E1," he said. "We'll go there and show you—once we get everything put back. Let's go." Getting Dora to leave the American corridor and enter the European side was like tempting a sugar addict with cookies.

"Hey," Ruthie said from the ledge, "I could ride in your pocket to the other corridor!"

Jack agreed and gently scooped her up and placed her in one of his roomy pockets at thigh level. Ruthie felt big fuzzy globs of lint beneath her feet and had to pull down on the top edge of the pocket to peer out.

Dora used her Art Institute key without hesitation. Jack had already stepped into Gallery 11 when Ruthie had the terrifying thought that the guard would notice that three people had gone in and only two were coming out! She ducked deeper in Jack's pocket.

"Where's Louis?" Ruthie heard Dora ask.

"Half-hour break, Ms. Pommeroy," a different voice answered. Dora let this guard know that they were doing research and swiftly opened the door to the European side. Ruthie told herself not to be so careless next time.

Once the corridor door had closed behind them, Ruthie called to Jack from his pocket, "I'd better get big again so we can shrink together." Otherwise—since having Dora become small was part of the plan—Dora would have to control the shrinking with Jack, and Ruthie didn't want to give her that opportunity. Jack lifted her from his pocket and set her on the ground. He bent down to the tiny Ruthie and she dropped the key into his open hand. The key returned to full size right in his palm, and Ruthie grew to her full size at the same time.

"Now, what's left?" Ruthie asked.

Dora took out a jade vase and a silver teapot from her leather bag.

"That's it?" The globe was not among the items. "Nothing left in the shopping bag?"

"That's all," Dora answered rather defensively. Ruthie guessed it must still be in the apartment Dora was decorating; they would have to figure out how to get it back.

"What rooms are these things from?" Ruthie asked.

"The teapot belongs in the English drawing room, E7, and the jade vase is from the Japanese room. Now can we please explore?" Dora was losing patience.

"How are you at climbing?" Jack reached into his pocket and pulled out the toothpick ladder.

Dora looked skeptical. "Climbing?"

"You said you wanted to explore. How else do you think we get to the ledge when we're small?" He attached the ladder.

"Couldn't we just use the stepladder?" she asked.

"We have to shrink together, and there's not enough room for three of us on it," Jack explained, giving the ladder a little tug to make sure it was secured. "I'm ready when you guys are."

They directed Dora to put everything back in her bag so the objects would shrink with her. Then Jack took the key from his pocket. Dora's eyes flickered with envy, as though she wished to grab the twinkling treasure for herself.

Ruthie reached out her right hand for Dora to hold while Jack put the key in her left palm, clasping his hand to hers. They had never tried having three people shrink at once and weren't really sure what would happen. Ruthie felt the breeze start up right away but it seemed to take a few seconds longer for everything to grow around them, as though the strength of the magic was diluted. When the shrinking was over, Dora looked around and gasped, cowering as she responded to the scale.

Standing on the floor in the corridor was very different from being up in the rooms or even on the ledge. First of all, it was much darker away from the glow of the rooms and the space loomed menacingly; a feeling of vulnerability was hard to fight off. Ruthie and Jack were used to it, Dora wasn't.

Jack took the leather bag from her. "Here, I'll carry this if you're not used to climbing." She smiled weakly at him.

Ruthie put Christina's key in her pocket and they began the five-story ascent. Secretly Ruthie felt a pang of sympathy for Dora, remembering the first time she had made this climb. After all, it felt like climbing up the side of the Grand Canyon, something Ruthie doubted she would have been brave enough to do before this magic adventure. She had conquered her fear and was now able to look down without queasiness. But Dora was frozen where she stood. Jack was in the lead, and he and Ruthie were more than halfway up by the time Dora finally took her first tentative steps toward the ladder. Then they heard her scream.

Out of the shadows appeared a mouse! Imagine coming into contact with a whiskered creature the size of a Volkswagen! Its nose twitched violently, and the little pink paws didn't look so cute at this size; the sharp claws were

longer than the tines on a fork. Baring its jagged teeth, it made an ear-piercing squeak, probably in fear itself. Dora and the mouse were inches apart, and it was hard to say who was more frightened. She screamed again and turned.

"It's the curse!" she shrieked. "Help!"

Jack said in a low voice so only Ruthie could hear, "Mice are nonaggressive herbivores." But aloud he called to Dora, "Run!"

The panicked woman zigged and zagged down the corridor, not looking behind her, and therefore not realizing the rodent had headed off in the opposite direction.

"No, run this way, to the ladder," Ruthie instructed. Dora finally changed tack and jumped onto the bottom rung. She clung to the ladder for dear life.

"That was horrible," she said through heaving breaths. "Did you see its teeth? It could have killed me!"

"You're safe now," Ruthie reassured her. But then to Jack she said, "Jack, do you think it really was the curse?"

"Might be," he said, continuing the climb. Ruthie followed.

"Hey, wait for me!" Dora yelled.

"We have to keep going. The sooner we get these things put back, the better," Jack called down. "Who knows what else might happen!"

Ruthie and Jack climbed onto the ledge while Dora was still near the bottom, trying to get the hang of climbing. They were near E7, where the teapot belonged, so they started toward the entrance of that room.

"Where are you? Don't leave me!" Dora yelled at them from the ladder.

"Don't worry. Keep climbing," Ruthie called out without stopping.

Together, they found the side room that led them to the open door of E7. "What do you remember about this room?" Jack asked.

"It's English, I think from the 1730s," Ruthie answered, gazing into the wood-paneled room. This was definitely one of Ruthie's favorite rooms; it looked both fancy and cozy at the same time. Near the elaborately carved mantel—over which hung a very large portrait of a woman and her dog—sat a big wingback chair covered in red and white fabric. She thought that would be the perfect place to curl up with a book. A tea set, missing its pot, sat on a small table between the chair and the fireplace.

"Do you think the room is alive?" Jack asked.

"I can't really tell. I don't hear anything." She glimpsed the stony white facade of another building out the window, but from where they stood it looked painted, not real.

"We'd better hurry," Ruthie said. "Dora's going to be up here any second."

Jack pulled the teapot from the bag.

"You can do it," Ruthie offered.

She watched Jack walk into the room—after he made sure no one was coming—and place the silver object next to the others in the set. Sure enough, the faraway bells chimed delicately, lasting only a few moments. Even standing off to the side in the doorway, Ruthie could sense the change in the room. It was as though a gentle breath sighed through it. She looked again at the view out the window, which had subtly changed; the building no longer looked painted, and shadows cast by clouds danced across it. A window next to the mantel was open a crack. They both heard the sounds from the street blow in on a breeze.

At that point, Jack should have turned and gone back to her, but he didn't. She watched him walk over to take a look at a chess set. The red and white ivory pieces, although perfect for the shrunk Jack, were incredibly tiny. He lifted up the king for Ruthie to see and called across the room to her, "This is awesome!"

"Watch out, Jack," she called to him from the doorway; she spied someone coming into view. There was a tall folding screen right next to him and he ducked behind it.

While Jack waited for his chance to exit, they both heard Dora, who was now near the top of the ladder and none too happy. Ruthie looked from the screen to the viewing window, not wanting to be left alone with Dora. She saw Jack peek out from behind the screen.

Dora's voice grew in volume as she made her way through the framework and into the side room where Ruthie stood.

"You promised me that I would get to learn all about the rooms and explore the past, not some horrible curse!" As she shouted at Ruthie in the little room, she stepped closer and closer to the entrance of the main room.

"Dora—" Ruthie began.

"No excuses! I know you're holding out on me—both of you." She turned toward the room. "Where is he?" She stormed into the room without checking the window.

"Dora, look out!" Ruthie called to her. But it was too late. She was standing in the middle of the room—face to face with a large head of a ten-year-old boy looking in at the room.

Through the glass, they heard him call to his friends, "Hey, look! This one has a hologram or something!" Dora stood stunned for a moment, then regained her senses and ran back to Ruthie just before two more boys joined the first. "It went off into the side room. It looked like a Barbie doll."

"Yeah, right, dude!" one said.

They heard the boys arguing as they moved away from the window.

Dora glared at Ruthie. "Why did you let me do that?"

"Dora, you have to be more careful," Ruthie said as evenly as she could.

"Yeah," Jack said as he ambled back into the side room. "You're gonna get us caught."

Dora took a deep breath. "All right—fine. I'll follow your lead."

"Good."

The jade vase was the last object left in Dora's bag. Soon, if everything went according to plan, Dora's thieving would be stopped and Ruthie would no longer have to bear the guilt of having confided in a thief.

···16···
THE STAKEOUT

JACK, STILL CARRYING DORA'S LEATHER bag, reached in and retrieved the vase. The three of them stood in the little side room adjacent to E31, the Japanese Room. Everything was just as it had been when Ruthie had removed the bento box and when Jack had replaced it; the room was too still, too quiet.

"Go ahead, Jack. It belongs on the low table right in front of the scroll painting," Ruthie said.

Jack stepped across the tatami mats and set the beautiful green vase in place. No sooner had he done so than the chiming of the magic wafted through the room on a breeze that came from the garden. Dora took a step back when she heard the sound.

"We were right," Jack said to Ruthie. "It was alive the first time."

"What are you talking about? What was that noise?" Dora asked.

"This vase is the object that animates the room," Ruthie answered.

"That's unbelievable!" Dora exclaimed.

Jack walked into the Zen garden, out of sight, while Ruthie stayed next to Dora.

"Dora, the bento box there." She pointed to Jack's box on the black lacquer table. "Did you write on the note inside it?"

"I was wondering when you'd ask. Yes, I did. When I opened the room from the glass front to study the miniatures, something about the box stood out to me." Ruthie could feel Dora's obsession as she continued. "When I found your note—I had to write back. I used a magnifying glass and a very sharp pencil. Several weeks went by. Then I read about you and Jack in the paper, about how you had found Mr. Bell's album. I knew you had to be the same kids. And then, as luck would have it, I met you that morning in the gallery."

Ruthie let her talk without interrupting or asking any more questions. It was clear she wasn't going to tell the entire truth about going to Mr. Bell's opening: Dora had needed to see what they looked like so she would recognize them in the museum. It wasn't luck at all that they had met. Dora had been betting on the fact that sooner or later she and Jack would show up in Gallery 11.

"I had already discovered that some of the miniatures weren't really miniatures at all, but valuable antiques that had found their way into the rooms. I had the problem that I already told you about, that some of them had grown in my bag, and they were sitting in my apartment until I could figure out how to shrink them and return them."

"Well, it's good that we've put them all back," Ruthie said, a meaningful tone in her voice.

Dora looked at her for a split second. "Don't you believe me?"

"There's still a globe missing from E6," Ruthie said. She saw a look flash across Dora's face.

"Oh, that. It was in my office, and a client insisted on having it. I've been planning on getting that back. Clients can be very demanding."

Now that Ruthie knew for certain that it was Dora who had written on the note, it was time to remove it from the room before anyone else came across it. "Wait here." Ruthie checked the viewing window and then rushed over to the bento box. She retrieved the letter just as Jack was coming back from the garden. "Do you still want to leave your box here?"

"Yeah. I like knowing that it's here. What do you think?" Ruthie nodded.

Back in the side room, Jack handed Dora her leather bag. "Here, you might as well take this now."

"Thank you." Dora looked at Ruthie and Jack for a couple of long moments. Then she said, "I would love to help you two understand what an opportunity you have here. No one has this sort of access to such treasures!"

Ruthie could hardly believe that Dora was still plotting

how to steal more objects! It was clear; Dora wasn't going to change her ways. But Ruthie played along. "Let's go to E1 and show Dora everything," she said in her most convincing voice.

"We'd better hurry," Jack called as he charged forward. "We don't have a lot of time."

As they approached the ladder, Jack stepped aside. "Dora, why don't you go first. That way you won't worry that we'll be leaving you behind, since we climb faster."

"Thank you," she responded.

When Dora was about ten rungs down Ruthie quietly took Duchess Christina's key from her pocket and grabbed Jack's hand. She tossed the key over the ledge, and together they jumped.

As Dora saw their two expanding figures fly by, she lost her footing and nearly fell. She dangled for several seconds until she was able to get her high heels on a toothpick again. "What are you doing?" she yelled.

"We don't really think you're the kind of person we can trust to keep the magic safe. Sorry, Dora," Ruthie said.

"But where are you going? How will I get big?" Dora screamed hysterically.

"When the museum closes"—Jack looked at his watch—"in about two hours, just slip under the door. You'll be full-sized before you get to the stairs," he said.

Ruthie couldn't resist adding, "Watch out for mice. And there are cockroaches too."

"Wait! Please, don't leave me here alone." They didn't even turn around again.

"You'll be sorry!" That was the last thing they heard Dora's tiny voice shriek at them as they unlocked the door and left her alone in the dark corridor, clinging to the ladder.

By the time they arrived at the apartment building where Dora lived (it had been easy to find—she was the only Pandora Pommeroy in the phone book), the police were already there with a search warrant. Ruthie and Jack ran from the bus stop and found Dr. Bell—as planned—standing near her car talking to one of the officers.

"Ruthie, Jack! How did it go?" she asked.

"Better than we planned!" Ruthie said.

"Piece of cake!" Jack echoed. "I think she'll show up here around five-thirty."

"Are you the two amateur detectives we owe thanks to?" the policeman asked.

"Officer Randolph, this is Jack Tucker, and this is Ruthie Stewart," Dr. Bell said.

"Pretty clever of you two to figure out who the art thief was and provide us with evidence."

"We got lucky," Jack said modestly.

"Officer Randolph just gave me some interesting news," Dr. Bell started. "The woman who had given the suspect the necklace as a tip came forward this morning. She'd been out of town, but as soon as she returned and read about it in the paper, she contacted the police. She had befriended the man, and he confided in her that he wanted to impress his girlfriend but didn't have enough money to buy her an expensive gift. She said she'd felt sorry for him, and she thought the necklace didn't suit her anyway. Can you believe it?"

"Some tip, huh?" Officer Randolph concluded. Then something seemed to occur to him, and he asked Jack and Ruthie, "How do you know she'll be here at five-thirty?"

Jack and Ruthie looked at each other, and Ruthie responded, "She's doing something at the Art Institute, and it closes at five."

"Well, you've been right about everything so far. We'll just expect her then." He walked away to confer with the other officers.

"The police were really knocked over when I took the video in," Dr. Bell told them. "I also showed them the photo evidence you gave me with the apples. It turns out that a couple of collectors who had recently hired her as a decorator began talking to each other about the thefts. They started getting suspicious and had spoken to one of the detectives on the case, but they had no hard evidence. Your video was exactly what they needed!"

"That's great!" Ruthie said.

"I bet we'll be in the papers again!" Jack added gleefully.

"All they need to do is search her apartment for the stolen property, and then they can arrest her," Dr. Bell explained.

Now it was hurry-up-and-wait time. At five-fifteen they got in Dr. Bell's car to watch.

"I almost forgot," Jack said, reaching into his backpack. "I swiped these from Dora's bag when I was out of sight in the Zen garden."

Ruthie looked at a set of keys in Jack's hand. "I wondered what you were doing back there." The keys were all labeled AIC, for the Art Institute of Chicago; one was the access door key, and a smaller one had a tag that said *TR Fronts*. "The key to the access door and the windows! Now for sure she'll never be able to steal from the rooms!"

At five-thirty Dora's car screeched to a halt in front of her building. She got out, slammed the door and stomped to the entrance.

Almost immediately, the three police officers followed her into the building.

"I wonder how long it will take," Dr. Bell asked. "I've never watched an arrest happen!"

Her question was answered quickly: about fifteen minutes after they'd gone in, the officers came out again, this time with a handcuffed Pandora Pommeroy in tow. She stood tall and still elegant-looking between the policemen, but the face of this woman who had once appeared so stylish and impressive was now transformed by equal parts of pride and anger. They watched in silence as the police put her in the back of the squad car and drove off.

Dr. Bell went with Ruthie and Jack back to Mrs. McVittie's and quickly told her everything. Then Ruthie's parents arrived, with Claire. Jack called his mom and invited her to

dinner at Mrs. McVittie's, and Dr. Bell stayed as well. Even Gabe showed up—Claire had phoned him.

"I can't believe it!" Claire exclaimed during dinner. "My little sister, the detective!"

Of course, not all of the story would be recounted publicly. But the part they could talk about, and the part that made the headlines, was amazing enough!

"There are going to be some very happy collectors in Chicago now that the real thief's been caught," Lydia said.

"So, Ruthie and Jack," Ruthie's father began, "when did you become suspicious of Dora?"

Jack answered, "At first she just seemed like a nice lady giving art lessons."

Ruthie thought about it for a minute. In hindsight there were a few moments during her drawing lessons that had made Ruthie wonder a little about Dora. "I should have known sooner. She sometimes seemed more interested in things than in people. That's never a good sign."

"But what was the deal with the apples?" Claire asked.

"We figure they're her signature," Jack answered. "You know—her calling card."

Then Ruthie felt a flash of insight. "Apples! Of course! Mom, isn't the French word for apple *pomme*?"

"Yes—oh, I see! And her name is Pommeroy. *Pommeraie* is the French word for an apple orchard!" her mother confirmed.

"I can't believe I didn't think of this before. No wonder I've been dreaming about apples all week!"

· · · 17 · · ·

A BLACKBIRD

THE NEXT DAY AFTER SCHOOL, Ruthie and Jack went to the police station to give statements and sign some papers. They agreed to be witnesses if there was a trial.

"You two have performed a great civic duty by helping us," Officer Randolph said. "She'll be in jail for quite a stretch. We checked her bank accounts; she's been making big bucks selling the stolen art. Personally, I think she's maybe a little crazy, that lady," he confided.

"Why do you think so?" Ruthie asked.

"She keeps talking about a curse that's been put on her. And something about a giant mouse!" He shook his head.

"Sounds crazy to me," Jack said.

"Me too," Ruthie agreed. "Crazy."

It turned out that Dora's apartment was filled with many stolen antiques, and it would take some time for the police to get everything back to the rightful owners. The collectors whose apartments she had decorated were very cooperative when they found out she had been selling stolen goods to them. Ruthie did a careful check of the Thorne Rooms against the photos in the catalogue, and as far as she could see, nothing other than the objects they already knew about seemed to be missing.

Getting the little silver box back from room E10 was easy—as far as the police were concerned, it belonged to Dr. Bell, since they had seen it stolen on Jack's surveillance video. It took several weeks to recover the globe. From Lydia's photograph of the collector's apartment Ruthie and Jack knew exactly where it was. Mrs. McVittie stepped up to claim it as hers, saying Dora had "borrowed" it from her shop. After she filed some official police documents, they eventually retrieved it (after all, they knew no one else could rightfully claim it). Ruthie and Jack planned to return it to the room where it belonged as soon as possible.

The staff at the museum was grateful to Ruthie and Jack for exposing the criminal in their midst. "I never really warmed up to that Ms. Pommeroy," the archivist told them later. "She was always so perfect, never a hair out of place. That's just not normal."

The story did make the newspapers, as Jack had predicted—the front page! "Sixth Graders At It Again; Use Spring Break to Catch Thief," one headline read. At both of their houses the voice mail was overloaded with messages from reporters. At Oakton, they were congratulated during morning announcements, and the whole school could be heard applauding the local heroes.

By Friday, Ruthie declared to Jack, "I'm kinda getting tired of all this, aren't you?"

"Don't worry. Everyone will forget by Monday." He was only off by a few days.

It was Dr. Bell who approached them about making a return trip to the rooms. Ever since the day they had come to her office and unleashed her memories, she had been pondering what it would feel like to experience the magic one more time. "I'd like to put the silver box back myself," she explained.

The following Sunday the weather was wonderful in the city, and a festival taking place in Grant Park ensured small crowds in Gallery 11.

"Stay really close to me, Dr. Bell, and keep your hand where I can grab it," Ruthie instructed. "It will happen fast. As soon as the shrinking stops, just go straight under the door."

"Are you sure I can do this? What if the magic doesn't work?" Dr. Bell asked, sounding worried.

Jack said, "It'll work. We've gotten pretty good at this."

"Just do what we do," Ruthie reassured her.

They didn't have to wait long; the guard had gone to stand at the entrance, facing away, and no visitors were anywhere near them.

"Okay," Jack said. Ruthie grabbed Dr. Bell's hand just

as Jack placed the key in Ruthie's other hand and held on tight. The magic worked beautifully. Quickly the three of them scooted under the door.

Caroline Bell laughed. "Incredible! That was great!" She stood up and looked around the immense corridor. Ruthie saw in Dr. Bell's face something of the little girl who had first discovered the magic. "I remember! It's coming back to me."

Ruthie and Jack waited, letting her have a moment to let it all sink in before Ruthie said, "Let's go to the ladder." She started off into the corridor. Jack and Dr. Bell followed, and soon they saw the ladder, still hanging near room E7.

"You two climbed the whole way up?" Dr. Bell said.

"One of us could get big and lift you, if you'd rather not climb it," Ruthie offered.

"No, I'm game." She walked closer and admired Jack's handiwork.

She was much more of a natural athlete than Dora, and wasn't wearing high heels, so the climb went smoothly. Once she was standing on the ledge, Dr. Bell looked around. "Wow. Now I remember what this felt like."

The silver box belonged in E10, a dining room from eighteenth-century England, which wasn't too far along the ledge. Ruthie, Jack and Dr. Bell climbed through the framework and found the entrance to the room, a heavy wooden door with a big golden knob. Fortunately the door was open halfway. Dr. Bell looked in first.

"Yes, this is the room," she said. "Will you come with me?"

"Sure," Ruthie and Jack said.

The three of them walked into the room. The pale green walls were covered in delicate white carvings, and most of the furniture was highlighted with gold. A statue of the goddess of the hunt, Diana, looked out from a wall niche.

"Do you remember where it goes?" Ruthie asked.

"Over there." Dr. Bell stepped onto the finely embroidered rug and walked past the dining table to the far side of the room, where a three-tiered table stood. She placed the silver box on it. As she did so, they all heard the faraway but omnipresent tinkling, like an enveloping whisper; it was gone before they could exhale. Next they noticed the subtle but unmistakable change that took place: sounds of life could be heard from outside the large window. The view was of a walled courtyard, with a tall, wrought-iron gate in the center. Caroline Bell turned just in time to see a blackbird swoop down and land on the gate, chirping furiously. Her jaw dropped.

"Am I really seeing what I think I'm seeing?"

"Yes!" Ruthie said. "But we'd better get out of here."

Outside the door, Dr. Bell still looked thunderstruck. "It can't be . . . it's not possible."

Jack and Ruthie explained to her what they'd learned about certain objects—the really old ones—animating the rooms. They told her about hearing the voice of Duchess

Christina of Milan, about Sophie and Thomas, and about Louisa and her family, and Phoebe from Charleston.

When they'd finished, Dr. Bell said, "I'd like you to take me to the room where you found my backpack. The room with the canopy bed."

"That's E17. Right this way," Ruthie said, taking the lead.

When they arrived at E17, the door to the room was open as usual and the "daylight" from the tall window streamed in, illuminating the rich surfaces of the room. And there was the canopy bed, fit for royalty. Dr. Bell looked in and Ruthie could hear the catch in her breathing.

"Oh my," she said. "I think I remember. . . . It was in the big cabinet, wasn't it?"

"Yes," Ruthie answered. "I almost didn't see it, it was so dark in there, but I was in the cabinet hiding from sight. When my eyes adjusted, there it was."

"I used to go in there, thinking it was my own little world. That nothing bad could happen." Dr. Bell choked up for a minute. "I'm going to walk in there for just a second, if you think it's okay."

"Go ahead. Just listen for voices in the gallery," Jack said.

Dr. Bell tiptoed into the room. She touched the silk of the bed, then walked to the cabinet and looked in. Jack and Ruthie watched from the doorway.

When she came back to them, her eyes were glassy with tears. "Can I tell you a secret?"

"Sure," Ruthie answered.

"I'm remembering everything now: when I left my backpack with the photo albums in that cabinet, it wasn't really an accident. I did it on purpose," she said.

"Why?" Ruthie asked.

"I missed my mother so badly. I thought that if I couldn't have her, I didn't want anyone else to have her either. I knew my dad was planning an exhibition of those photos, and it felt like I would be sharing the only thing left of her. If I'd been a little older, I would have realized how much more I had to lose by hiding the album. But now I—my father and I—we have it back, thanks to you."

She sighed deeply.

"Thank you both so much," she said, smiling again. "I think we can leave now. That was good for me."

"I'm glad," Ruthie said. "But before we go, I want to check one more thing."

· · · 18 · · ·
THE DEAD LETTER

JACK AND DR. BELL FOLLOWED Ruthie along the ledge. "I've been thinking about Louisa and her family photo album," she said. "I think we should take a look at it, to see if the pages have been filled in."

"Good idea!" Jack said, already turning toward E27.

When they reached the room, Ruthie stepped through the framework and into the roof garden. She looked through the door into the room. The moment was right; she grabbed the album from where it rested on the coffee table and was out again.

"Let's see it!" Jack said excitedly. They thumbed through the first half quickly until they found the photograph that had been the last one, of the Meyer family in front of 7, rue Le Tasse. There were Louisa, her parents and Jacob, all smiling for the camera.

"Turn the page, Jack." Ruthie was too nervous to do it herself.

"Oh," Jack said, seeing the next page.

The album was just as it had been before, with dozens of empty pages. There were no new photographs—and no proof that the Meyer family had left Paris! Ruthie put her hand to her mouth, like a dam to stop the emotion that was about to flood out of her.

"Hey, don't worry," Jack said. "This doesn't mean anything. They couldn't take much with them; they probably left this behind."

"I suppose," Ruthie said. "But I just wanted to know for sure."

"Maybe you two could do some genealogical research and find out what happened to them," Dr. Bell suggested.

Ruthie nodded, trying to cling to some hope. "We could also check the Thorne Room archives to see if Mrs. Thorne left any notes about this album." She tried to sound optimistic, but worry remained in her voice.

They left the rooms by the usual route, going halfway under the door, waiting for the coast to be clear and then coming all the way out. Holding Jack's hand, Ruthie dropped the key to the floor. In a moment the three of them stood in the alcove at full size as though nothing at all had happened.

At the front door to the museum, Ruthie felt her

phone vibrate in her pocket. The caller ID showed it was Mrs. McVittie.

"Hello?" Ruthie answered. "Sure, why? . . . Okay." She hung up. "Hmmm. Mrs. McVittie wants us to come over, Jack. Right now. She wouldn't say why."

Jack shrugged. "Okay."

"I have a question," Dr. Bell began as they walked down the steps outside the museum. "If Dora Pommeroy had stolen the key, how did you shrink?"

Jack looked around to see if anyone would notice and then took the dimly glowing square out of his pocket. "With this. It works just like the key. We don't know what it is, though."

"May I?" Dr. Bell was about to lift the square from his palm but stopped. "Will it make me shrink?"

"Not out here," Jack explained. "You have to be close to the rooms."

She picked up the square. "Hmmm, warm, isn't it?" She observed how it flashed in the sunlight. "I know what this is. It's a slave token, a tag."

"A what?" Ruthie asked.

"It's a tag that slaves in a few places in the South were required to wear. *C-h-a-r* must be Charleston, South Carolina, and *v-a-n-t* is probably *servant*. The numbers are most likely the slave's number and the year the tag was made. I think they were worn around the neck."

"Whoa!" Jack exclaimed.

"Maybe that's why we met Phoebe! I bet this belonged to her!" Ruthie declared.

"They're highly collectible. Some families who are descended from slaves have them, often kept in family Bibles through the generations. You don't see them very often. If you need any help researching the tag, I know some people." Dr. Bell looked at the tag some more before handing it back to Jack. Then she hugged them both and said goodbye. "And thanks again for today. It was . . . amazing." She hailed a cab and hopped in.

They stood on the sidewalk looking at the metal square—the slave tag. In spite of its rough appearance, Ruthie and Jack had assumed that it must be something of importance to have been imbued with the magic. The key had come from a young woman of the nobility, a duchess; this tag had come from someone on the lowest rungs of the social ladder. So how could a slave have acquired this power? And why?

"I wonder how it ended up in the beaded bag," Ruthie said.

Jack shook his head. "Just when we get a bunch of puzzles solved, there's something else to figure out!"

Mrs. McVittie opened the door to her apartment and ushered them in. "Darlings, look! This was in yesterday's mail. I only just opened it."

She handed them a sheet of paper with the emblem of

the U.S. Postal Service on the letterhead. It was a letter of several paragraphs, but the most important part said:

> We at the postal service pride ourselves on providing the best mail delivery in the world, and yet not every letter finds its way to its addressee. Our inspectors periodically review the contents of the Dead Letter Office so that no accurately addressed letter is overlooked. Once in a great while, the post office comes across a letter incorrectly deemed "dead." We have no explanation as to how this letter—with a clear and accurate address—came to be labeled as such, or how it sat unnoticed all these decades. We are happy to deliver it to you now with our heartfelt apologies for any inconvenience from the significant delay.

"What letter?" Ruthie asked, thoroughly perplexed. Mrs. McVittie handed an envelope to her.

It was yellowed with age, addressed in perfect script:

Miss R. Stewart,
in care of Minerva McVittie,
408 Walnut St., Chicago, Illinois, U.S.A.

The postmark read 1937!

"Look on the back," Mrs. McVittie said.

Ruthie turned it over. In the same lovely handwriting it read:

Louisa Meyer, 7, rue Le Tasse, Paris, France

"It's addressed to you, dear. Open it!" Mrs. McVittie urged. She handed Ruthie a letter opener. Ruthie made the slit and pulled out a letter, folded once.

23 June 1937

Dear Ruthie,

I was so happy you met my family yesterday. I was worried I might not see you again. I hope your trip back to America was smooth, and perhaps this letter will be waiting for you after your journey home.

As I write to you, my family is about to board the SS Normandie. We will arrive in New York in four days! Father decided we will stay with our cousins in Brooklyn until we can return to our home in Berlin someday. We couldn't pack everything, but I have Frieda, and my mother says this will be a big adventure. My brother is very excited, but I must tell you, had it not been for meeting you and Jack, I would be sad. Knowing that I might make a friend like you or that perhaps we could visit each other makes me less homesick.

Please write to me in care of the Ginsburg family, 124 Hicks St., Brooklyn, New York.

Yours truly,
Louisa Meyer

"I can't believe it! How . . ." Ruthie was so astounded she couldn't even finish her sentence. "It couldn't have been sitting there for seventy years; wouldn't the post office have found it a long time ago?"

"It hasn't been there that long. Think about it," Jack said. "It probably just appeared there—not long after we met her family. That would have been after last Saturday, right?"

"Like Sophie's journal—how the last pages were filled in after we met her and warned her about the French Revolution!" Ruthie felt goose bumps all over.

"Exactly," Jack concluded. "That is so cool!"

"You two saved her life," Ms. McVittie said.

Ruthie read the letter from Louisa several more times, wondering what kind of life Louisa had had after the photo album ended. She felt elated and relieved. They had protected the Thorne Rooms from Pandora Pommeroy, and they had succeeded in convincing Louisa and her family to leave Europe. Together, she and Jack had done the right thing. Ruthie thought about Phoebe; giving her the notebook and pencils was such a small gesture. Could she and Jack do more for her?

For safekeeping, Ruthie left the letter from Louisa in a special wooden box in Mrs. McVittie's guest room, unable to imagine how she would explain such a letter if anyone in her family was to find it.

But the key and now the slave tag—what should they do with them? Ruthie looked at the two side by side in the palm of her hand, one elaborate, the other plain, both emitting their unusual sparkle. They didn't belong to her or to Jack, but Ruthie had a feeling that they were trying to tell her something, as though some secret still charged their glittering beauty.

"What do you think, Jack?" Ruthie asked him, the lid of the box still open. "We can't keep them forever."

He grinned. "We'll figure out where to return them. Soon. Okay?"

"Okay!" And with that, she dropped them into the box and shut the lid.

Room E27, French Library of the Modern Period. Paris of 1937 can be seen outside, including a view of the Eiffel Tower. Louisa's family album sits on the low round table.

AUTHOR'S NOTE

IN A BOOK LIKE THIS, readers may wonder where fantasy stops and historical fact starts. It's a very good question. Almost all of the characters here, like those in my previous book, *The Sixty-Eight Rooms,* came from my imagination. Ruthie and Jack, Mrs. McVittie and Dr. Caroline Bell, Louisa and Phoebe—even Dora Pommeroy—are invented. But as every writer understands, they are created out of snippets from lots of people in my life.

Amelia Earhart was, of course, a real person whose life was filled with adventure. The French held her in high regard and awarded her the *Légion d'Honneur,* the highest honor bestowed in France. This medal was given to her after her successful transatlantic flight in 1932. She made that flight in the Red Vega, a model of which I imagined Jack receiving from the souvenir vendor. Earhart made her ill-fated flight exactly at the time that Ruthie and Jack visited Paris—early summer in 1937.

The scene I describe outside Room E27 is historically accurate. One can find documentary photographs of the Exposition Universelle, and even archival film footage on YouTube. In 1937, Europe was on the brink of World War II, and thousands of people had been and would continue to be displaced from their homes and countries, the way Louisa and her family were.

Phoebe is a character whom I imagined living in Charleston, South Carolina, long before the Civil War. The object identified as a "slave tag" is a real remnant from that era in Charleston.

Dora—Pandora Pommeroy—is an invented character, to be sure, but her name comes from Greek mythology. The Pandora of myth was a woman on whom the gods had bestowed great gifts. She opened a box that humans were forbidden to open, and let all the evils of the world escape.

I have imagined my story in the historical contexts prompted by the Thorne Rooms. I would suggest to any reader interested in or inspired by history to learn all you can and imagine yourself in faraway times and places. It may change your perspective on your own world.

ACKNOWLEDGMENTS

TO MY WONDERFUL FAMILY—Jonathan, Maya, Noni and Henry. You know why. *Merci beaucoup!*

To my sister, Emilie Nichols, and my best friend, Anne Slichter, thanks for happy diversions and support along the way.

Thank you to Mican Morgan, the curator of the Thorne Rooms, for answering my questions and for saying when asked by a reporter that Ruthie and Jack's adventures were only "a little naughty."

I'm grateful to Professor Henry Louis Gates Jr. for answering my questions about historical language usage.

Huge thanks to Gail Hochman, my agent, who takes such great care of everyone she works with.

Finally, I have written a lot about magic in this story. But my wonderful editor, Shana Corey, performed the real magic. She is tireless, patient and talented. She has my deepest gratitude.

ABOUT THE AUTHOR

MARIANNE MALONE is an artist, a former art teacher, and the cofounder of the Campus Middle School for Girls in Urbana, Illinois. She is also the mother of three grown children. Marianne's first book for children, *The Sixty-Eight Rooms,* was named a Chicago Public Library Best of the Best Book and a *Parents' Choice* Recommended Award Winner.

ABOUT THE ILLUSTRATOR

GREG CALL began his career in advertising before becoming a full-time illustrator. He works in various media for clients in music, entertainment, and publishing. Greg lives with his wife and two children in northwestern Montana, where he sculpts, paints, illustrates, and (deadlines permitting) enjoys the great outdoors with his family.

DON'T MISS THE NEXT
SIXTY-EIGHT ROOMS ADVENTURE!

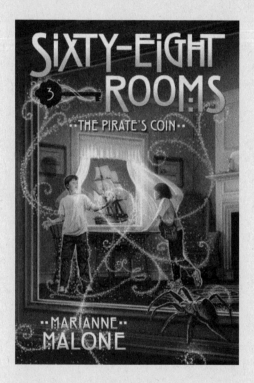

TURN THE PAGE FOR A PREVIEW!

THE CLEMENTINE

"DO YOU THINK HE'S OUT here?" Jack wondered, looking out from the porch.

"I think . . . it's possible. It depends on what the date is," Ruthie answered, not wanting to get his hopes up.

"If this is before the Revolutionary War," Jack said thoughtfully, "Massachusetts wasn't a state yet; it was still a colony. It would be good to know if we were about to walk into a Revolutionary War battle or something." Jack actually sounded like that wouldn't be such a bad thing.

They opened the gate and stepped out onto the road. A sign posted on a nearby façade read *Main Street*. They saw women carrying baskets laden with various supplies, and men pushing handcarts filled with wood, hay and piles of stuffed burlap sacks. No one stared at them since their clothing was perfectly authentic. Passing by a building, they heard the clank of metal on metal and looked in the broad doorway to see a blacksmith at work making horseshoes. Other wrought-iron objects such as pots and pans hung from the ceiling.

"Perfect," Ruthie said, noticing the next building. Through the rippled glass windowpanes they could see shelves lining the walls from floor to ceiling. It was a general store. Ruthie spied a stack of newspapers inside. She crossed the threshold to take a closer look.

"The *Boston Gazette*," she said to Jack. "June seventeenth, 1753! There's our answer."

"And what is your question?" A man's voice from behind the counter startled them.

Ruthie hadn't seen him and wished she had spoken more softly, but Jack said, "We were wondering if you sold the paper here."

"So I see," the man behind the counter said. "Visiting?"

"That's right," Ruthie replied.

"From where?" the man asked. He was dressed just like pictures they'd seen of Ben Franklin, complete with wire-rimmed glasses that he peered over as he gave Ruthie and Jack a stern glance.

"Boston," Jack answered right off.

"Do you want to purchase the *Gazette*?"

"Um. No. We were just looking at the front page," Ruthie said.

"I'll have no loitering in this establishment! Off with you both!"

"At least we know the date," Ruthie remarked once they were out in the street again. "Ten years after the date on your coin!"

Jack pulled the coin from a pocket in his vest. It flashed at him. "I'm gonna ask that man . . . ," Jack began, and headed back into the store before he finished his sentence.

Ruthie wasn't sure whatever he planned to ask was a good idea, but talking Jack out of it would have been next to impossible. So she followed him in.

"Excuse me, sir," Jack started.

The man was placing jars on a shelf. "Yes?"

"Can you tell me where to find Jack Norfleet?"

The man spun around to face them. "Why?"

"It's personal," Jack answered boldly.

"Luck be with you if you have business with a pirate!" He returned to his task. "Down at the harbor."

This news meant everything to Jack. They raced out the door and down the street, kicking up sandy dirt with every step.

They approached a cross street and Jack looked down toward the waterfront. "Let's go there." As soon as he spoke, the coin pulsed brighter. "Must be the right way!" he said.

Ruthie hustled to keep up with Jack, who, just as he had said before, seemed to be being tugged in that direction. The oceanfront was only a couple of hundred yards in front of them and the closer they got the more they could see of the busy harbor. Men worked on ships of all sizes and shapes; horse-pulled carts laden with supplies traveled on the road leading to the water.

They were almost there when Jack stopped in his tracks. "There she is! The *Avenger*!" He quickened his pace like someone possessed.

The ship was off to the left, not in the center of the harbor activity. It was large, with two tall masts, each holding three rectangular sails; behind them was a shorter mast with a single sail. Three smaller, triangular sails set at an angle were at the front and one odd-shaped sail was at the very rear of the ship. A long pointed rod jutted out from the prow like the sword of a swordfish.

Nearing the ship, Ruthie saw the name first: not *Avenger*, but rather *Clementine*, painted on the wood boards of the bow.

Jack saw it too. "But . . . it looked just like the one on the mantel."

"Let's go closer," Ruthie encouraged.

Ruthie only knew the boats she had seen harbored in Lake Michigan—motorboats, small yachts, sailboats for recreation. She'd never seen one as impressive as this before. It bobbed in the water, the sails puffed up by the gentle breeze.

Close to where they stood, near a pier that stretched out into the water, was a small, shingled structure with a sign over the door. Jack was still looking in the direction of the tall ship when Ruthie read the sign.

In clear black lettering it said:

JACK NORFLEET, SHIPWRIGHT

"Jack! Look! We found him!" She felt something close to the electric tingling that Jack had been feeling since the first time they had neared room A12.

The coin flickered like a tiny flame in Jack's palm. He put it back in his pocket and without hesitating lifted his hand to knock on the door.

"Wait!" Ruthie cautioned. "The man in the store . . . he didn't seem to think this was such a good idea. What if Jack Norfleet's—you know—not nice?"

"Only one way to find out," Jack said. He rapped on the door.

They waited but there was no response. It was a very small building, barely bigger than a shack, so if anyone were inside, they would surely have heard the knock.

"No one's there." Jack's voice was heavy with disappointment.

"Let's walk on the pier. Maybe we'll see him."

"Might as well," Jack agreed glumly.

The *Clementine* was moored to the pier by thick ropes tied to clusters of sturdy pylons sunk in the water. They walked along, getting a good close-up look at the ship and hearing the steady creaking of its timbers as it rose and fell with the waves. From this vantage point the white sails seemed even taller against the blue sky.

"It's beautiful," Ruthie said.

"Aye! That she is!" a voice behind them said. "The finest in the harbor."

Ruthie and Jack turned to see a woman who had just approached. She was young, perhaps about college age, Ruthie guessed, wearing a dark green dress edged with crisp white lace. She gazed at the *Clementine*.

"Hello," Ruthie said. "Do you know where we might find Jack Norfleet?"

"More than a chance he's on board. He doesn't venture forth often," the woman replied.

"Do you know him?" Ruthie asked.

"Only his reputation—which bridles my desire to meet him."

"What do you mean?" Jack responded.

"It is said his temper is easily kindled," the woman began. "I am therefore cautious to make his acquaintance, much as I wish to. I'm eager to convey to him the regard I have for his ship, how much pleasure it gives me each time I pass by." The breeze blew and filled the sails into graceful arcs curving outward from the masts high above them. "Some stay far away from him, but I think a man who builds ships like this must be of good character. The commonly held opinion cannot be the summary of him."

"So you've never met him?" Ruthie hoped she understood this eighteenth-century English correctly.

"In course I hope to, but my daring fails me in proportion to my esteem of his work."

Ruthie sensed herself translating as this woman spoke: *She is intimidated because his work is so impressive.* Jack seemed to understand.

"You're right. It's a great-looking ship," he agreed enthusiastically.

"Forgive my manners." The woman made a slight curtsy. "I'm Miss Wilshire."

"I'm Ruthie Stewart."

"Jack Tucker. Pleased to meet you."

"And I you." She smiled. "You don't live here?"

"Boston," Jack replied.

"I shall wait here while you find Mr. Norfleet. I should love an estimation of his mood. Perhaps today I will finally meet him—if you find him in agreeable temper."

"Sure. We'll let you know," Jack said. He turned and advanced toward the tall ship.

Suddenly a board shot out in front of them, landing on the pier a few paces ahead. It was a plank with horizontal struts used for getting on and off the boat. Someone on board the ship had hoisted it out from the deck.

"Avast!" a voice shouted at them. "Have you business here?"

They looked up and saw a man dressed in brown canvas pants, a loose white shirt and a dark vest, unbuttoned. He wore a heavy leather belt with several knives and daggers hanging off it. His hair was long and pulled back in a ponytail, and a bandanna-like scarf was wrapped around his head. He didn't exactly have a beard but he wasn't clean-shaven. One word shot through Ruthie's mind: *pirate!*